THE
ADVENTURESS

THE
ADVENTURESS

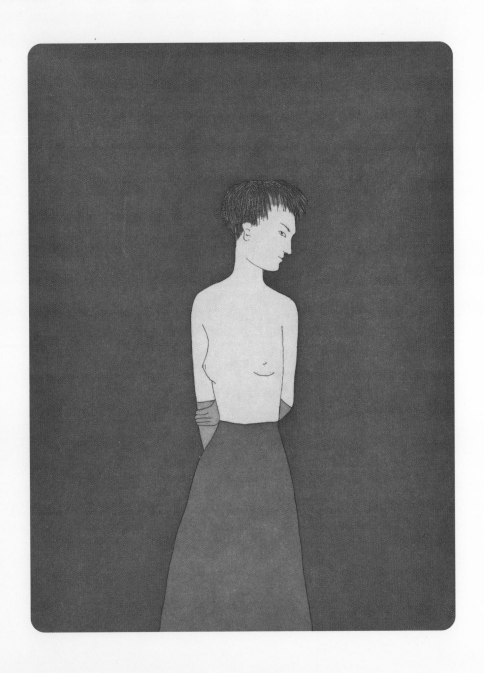

Audrey Niffenegger

Abrams
New York

Editor: Tamar Brazis
Designer: Celina Carvalho
Production Manager: Kaija Markoe

Library of Congress Cataloging-in-Publication Data:

Niffenegger, Audrey.
The adventuress / by Audrey Niffenegger.
p. cm.
ISBN 10: 0-8109-7052-X
ISBN 13: 978-0-8109-7052-6
I. Title.

PS3564.I362A66 2006
813'.54—dc22
2005030357

Printed and bound in China
10 9 8 7 6 5 4 3 2 1

HNA ■■■■■
harry n. abrams, inc.
a subsidiary of La Martinière Groupe

115 West 18th Street
New York, NY 10011
www.hnabooks.com

For Lisa Ann Gurr
and
Lawrence and
Patricia Niffenegger

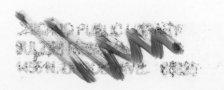

Introduction:

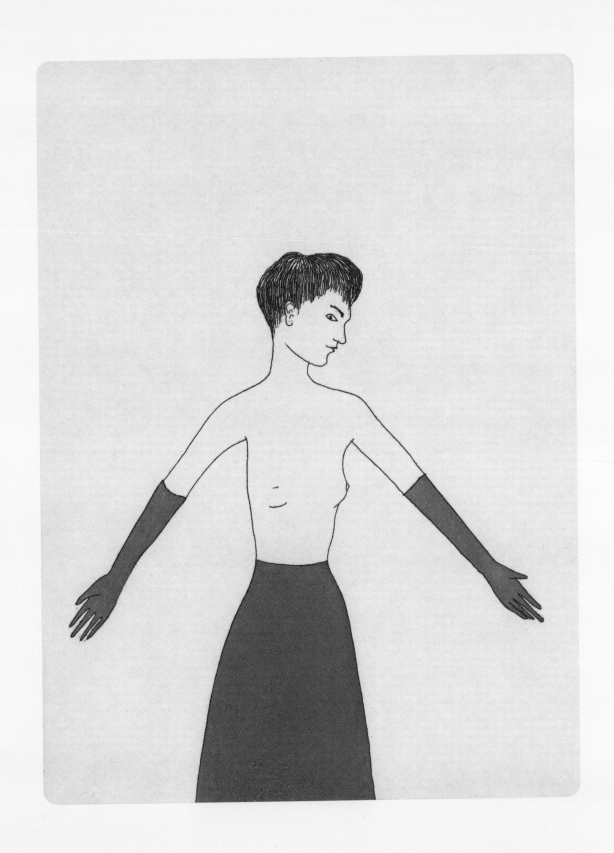

Evolution:
Her father was an alchemist;
He created her himself.
Of what, he would not say.

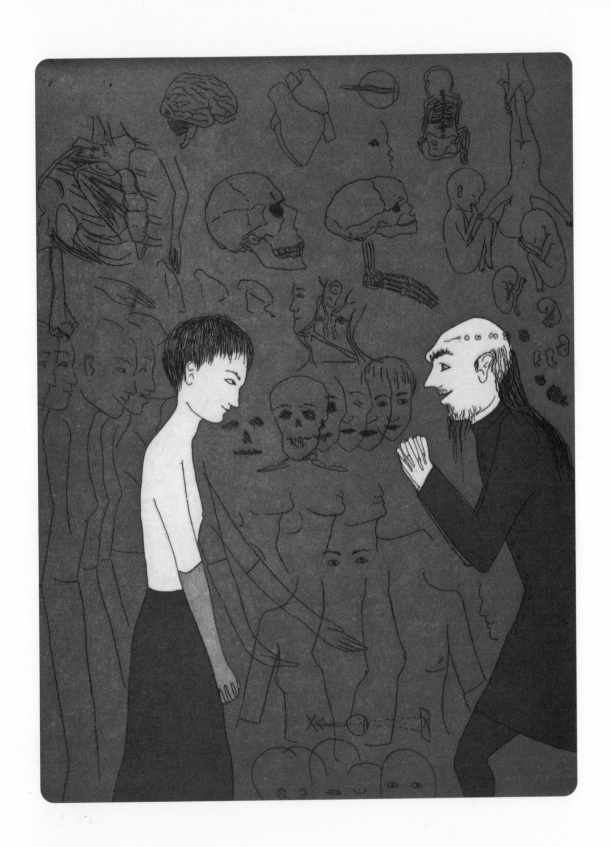

Instruction:

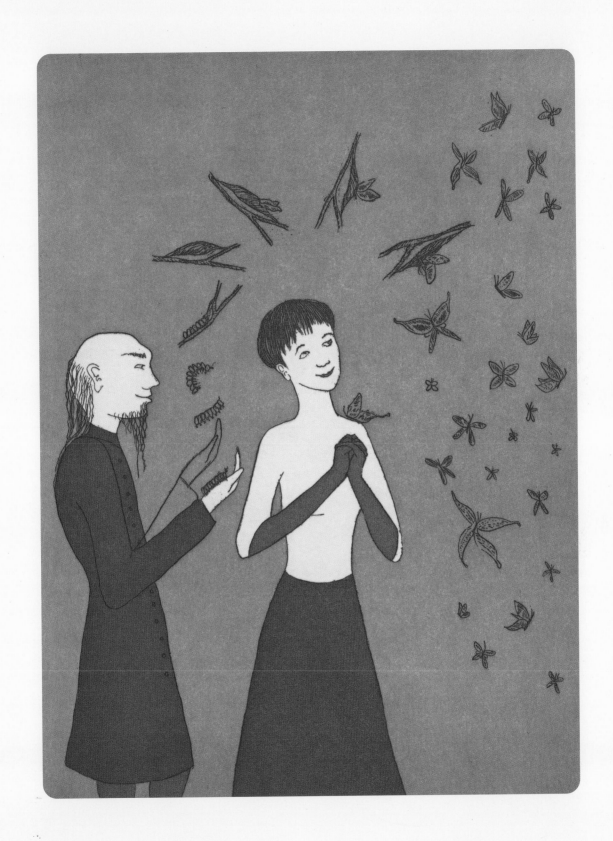

Her companions were the other
Creatures the alchemist had created.

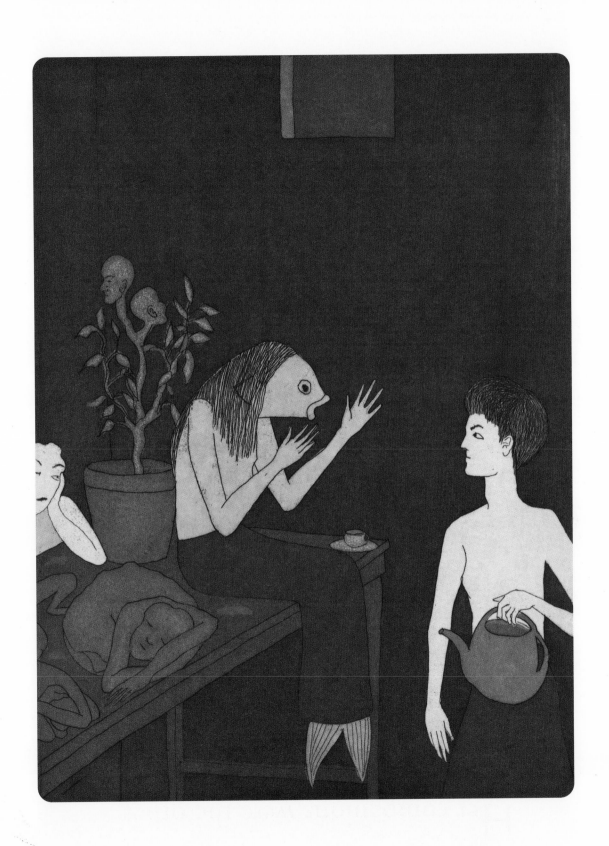

One day she stood at the window

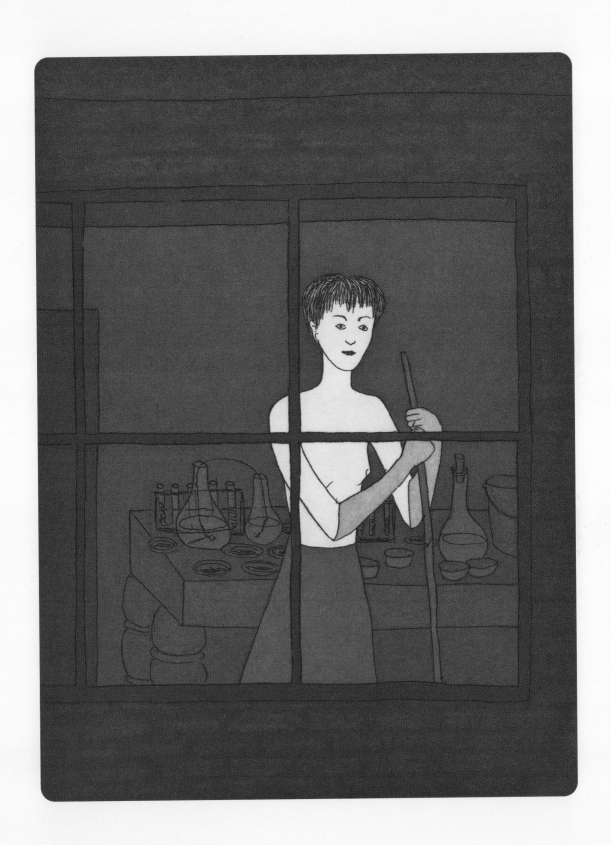

And was espied by the powerful Baron von K., who desired her.

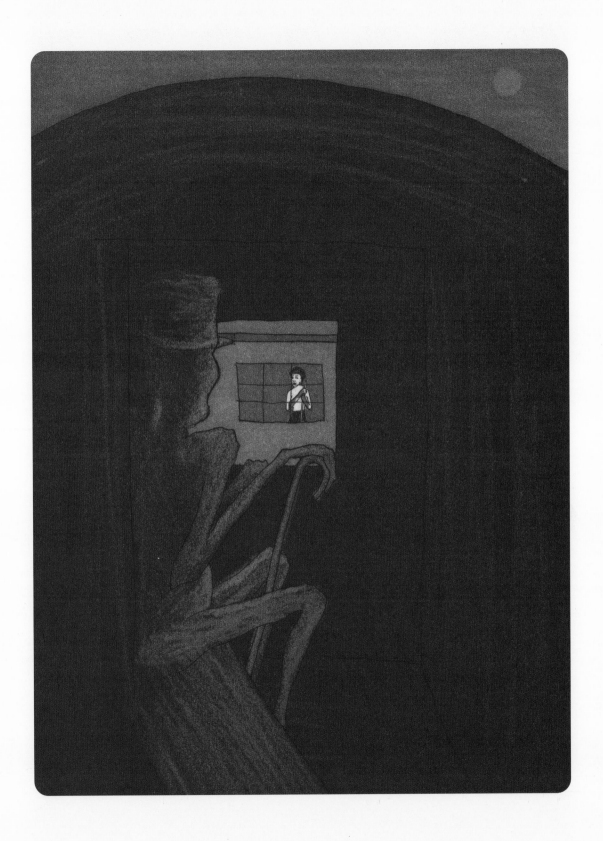

Soon after this, she was carried off

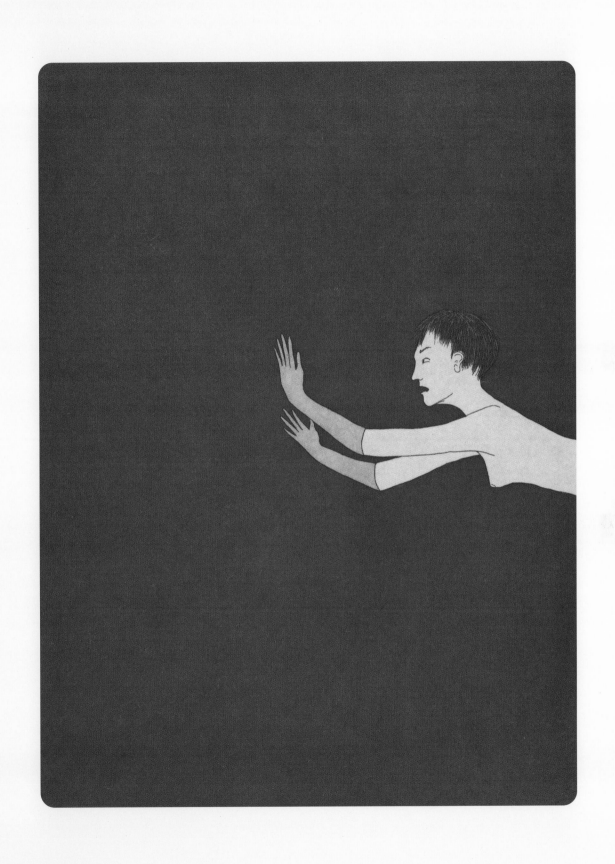

And taken away.

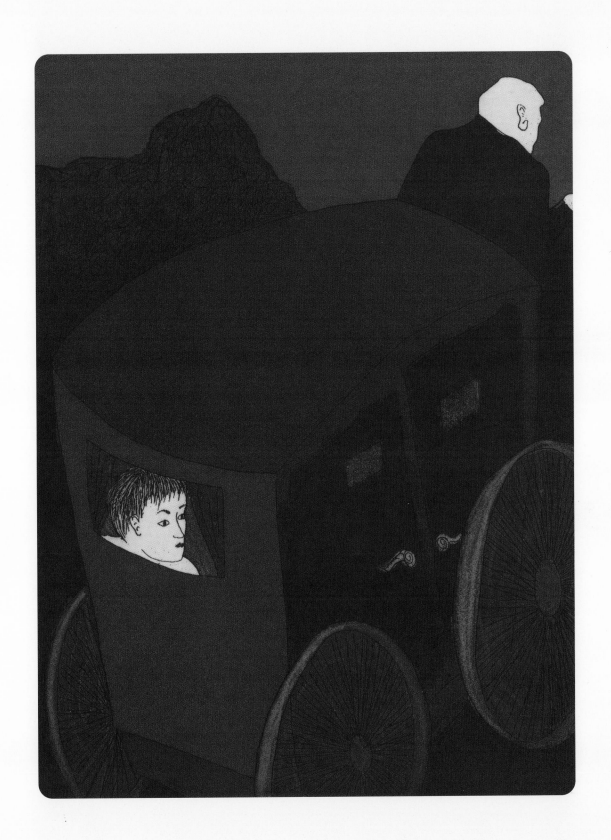

Her arrival at the castle
Of the Baron von K.:

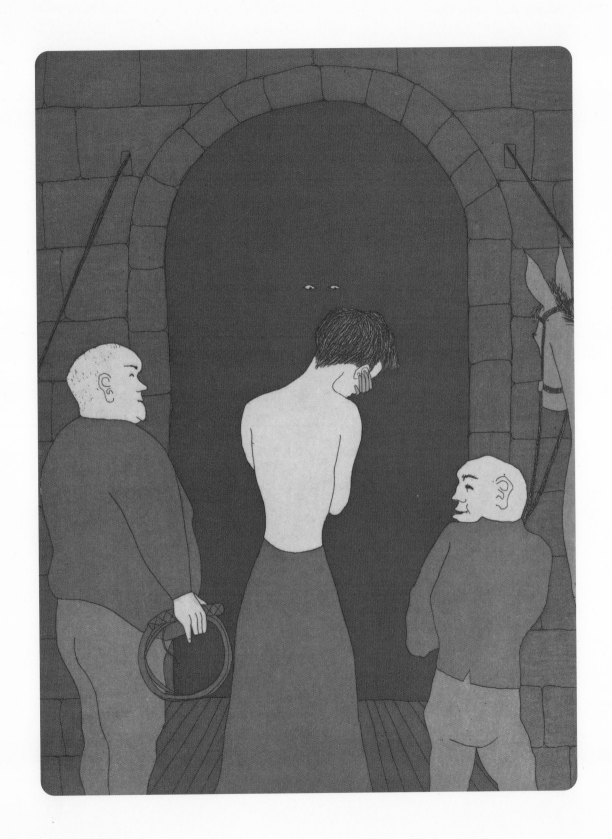

She was arrayed as a bride.

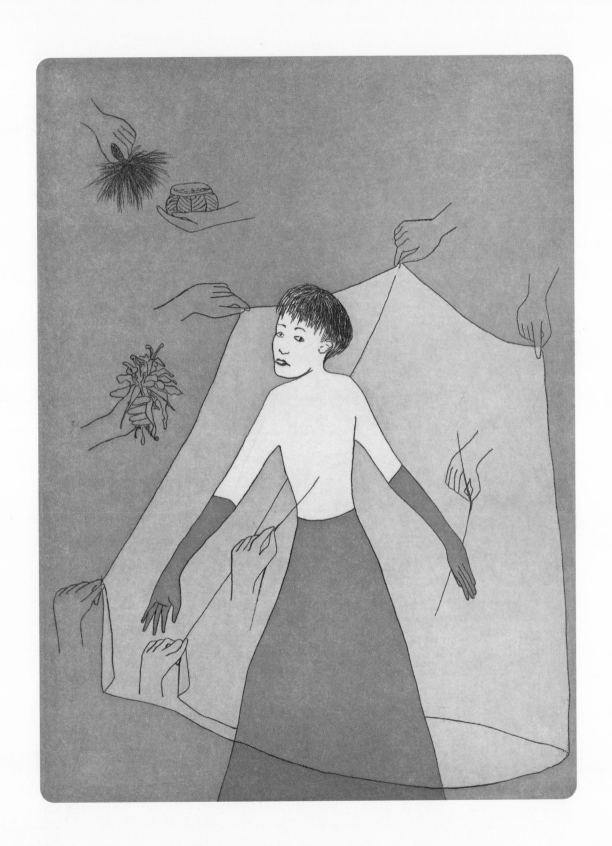

She found herself, then,
In a church
Amid a sea of eyes.

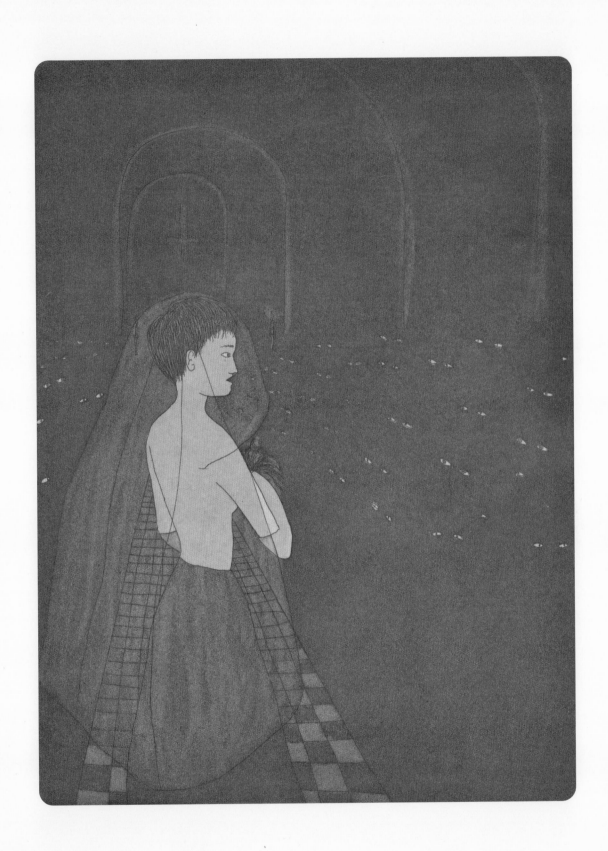

The wedding:

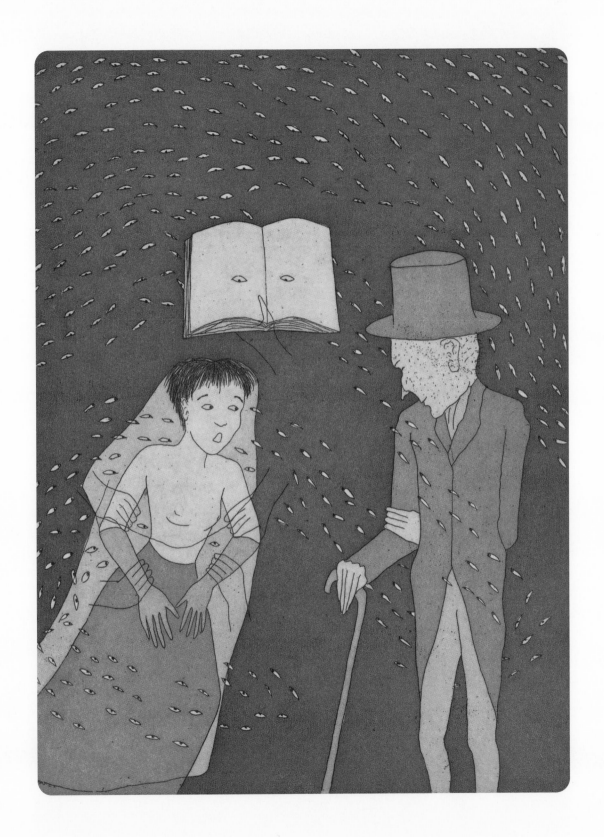

Revelry:

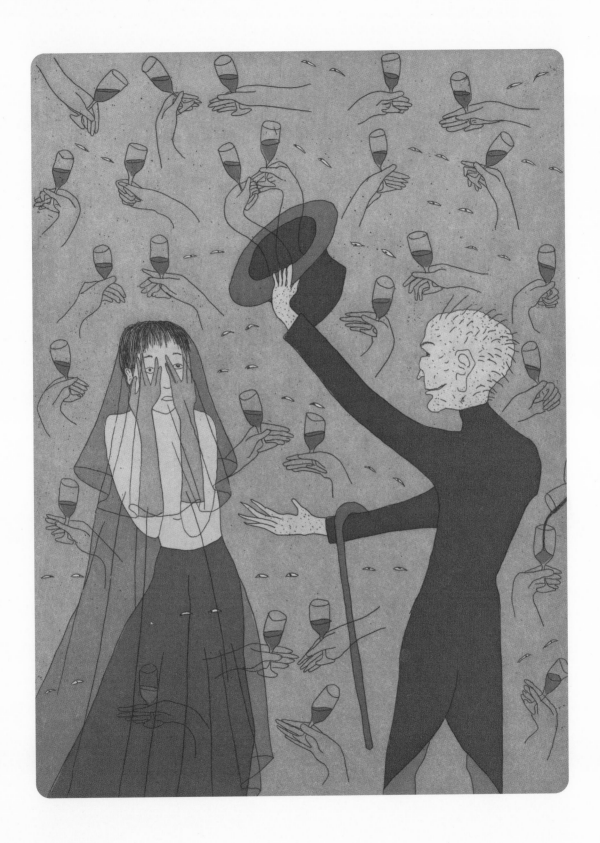

She was carried across the threshold.

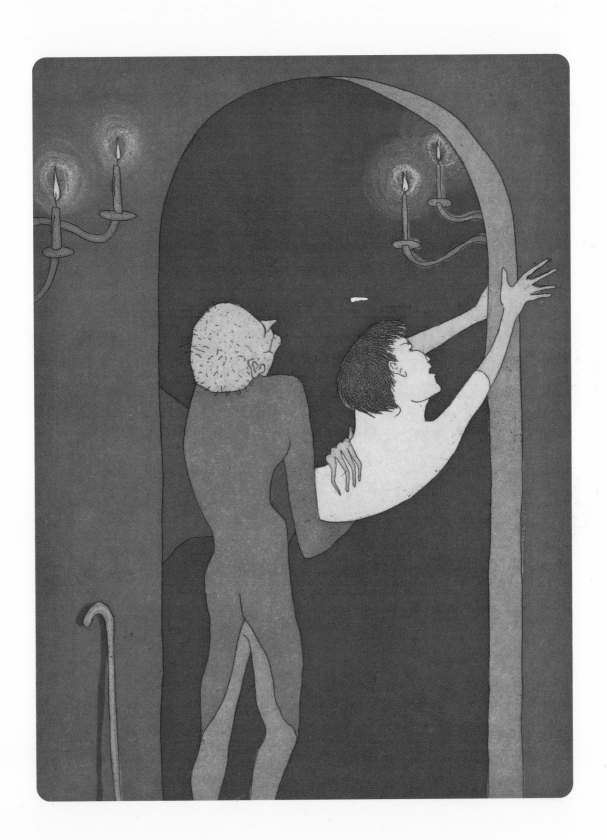

The honeymoon:

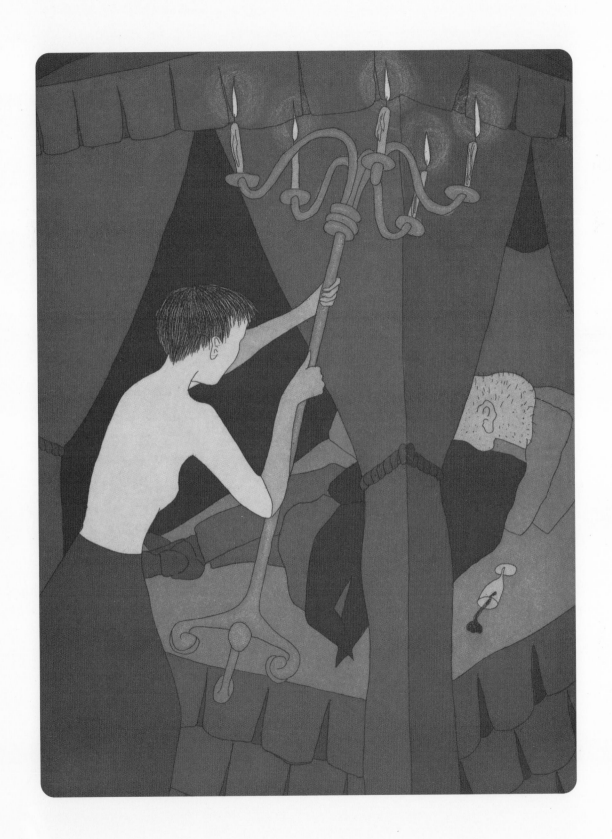

Running away, running away,
Running while *everything* burned:

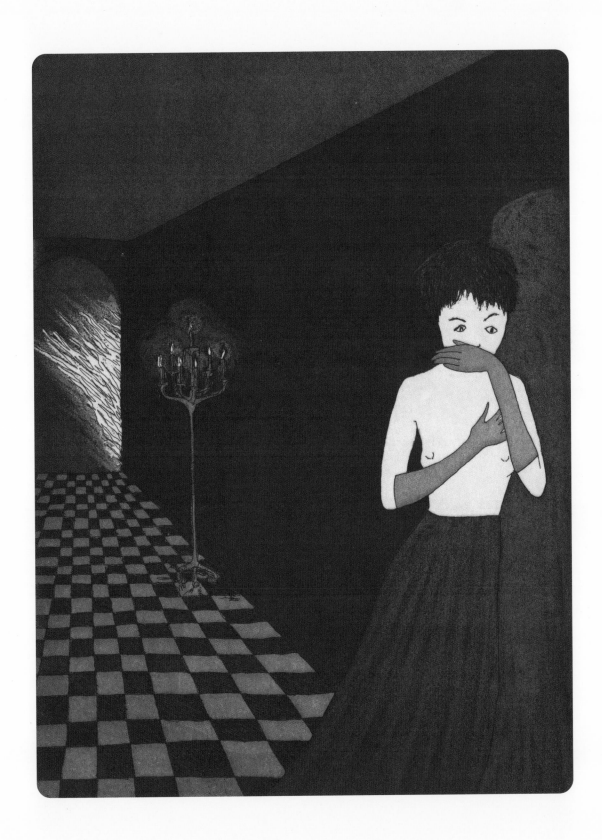

What to do?

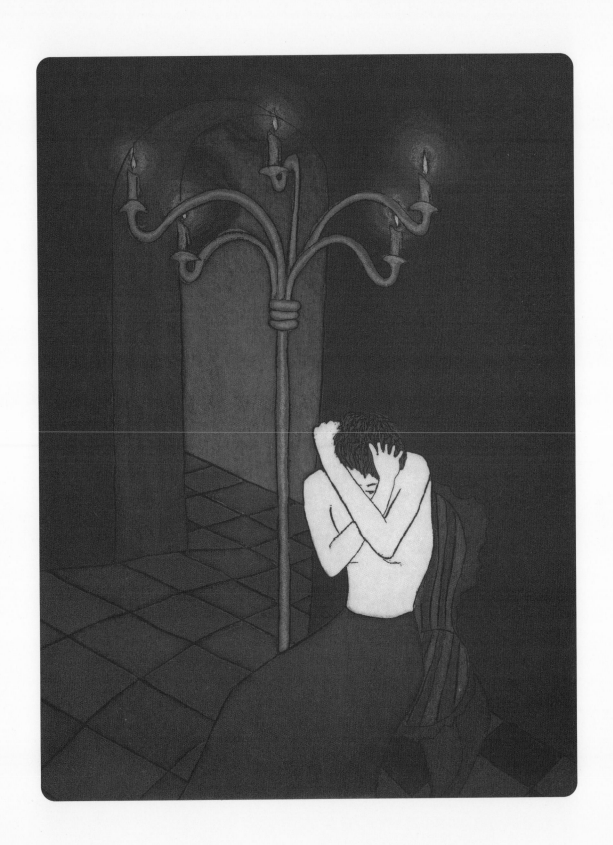

Running away:

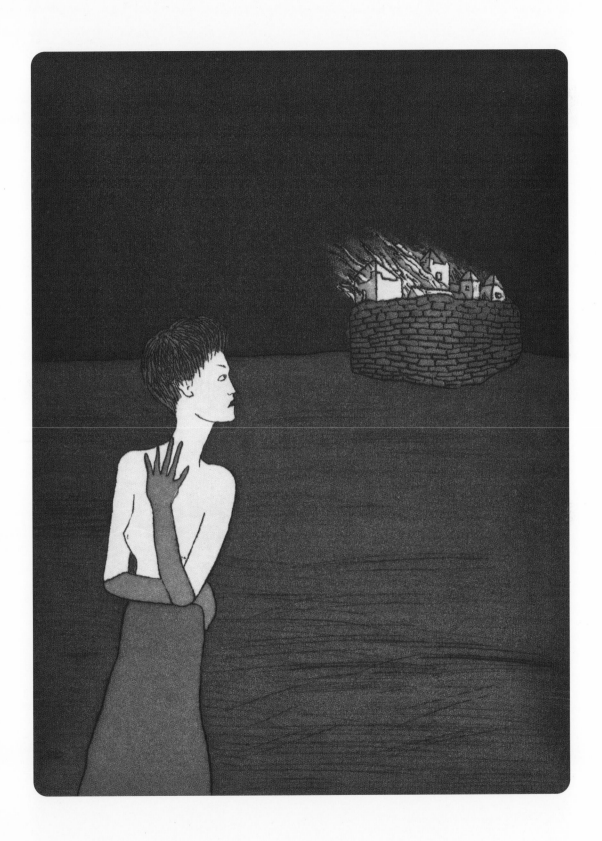

She was overtaken by horsemen.

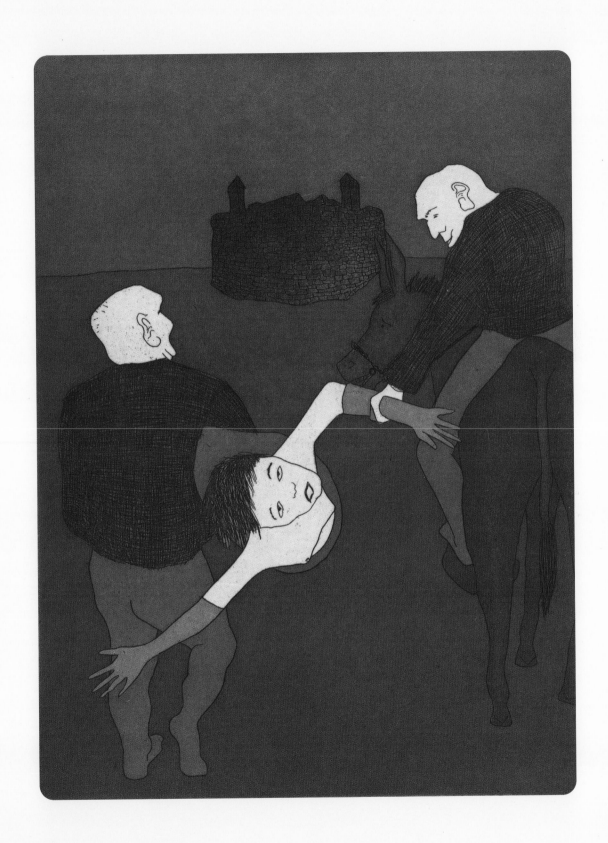

Tried:

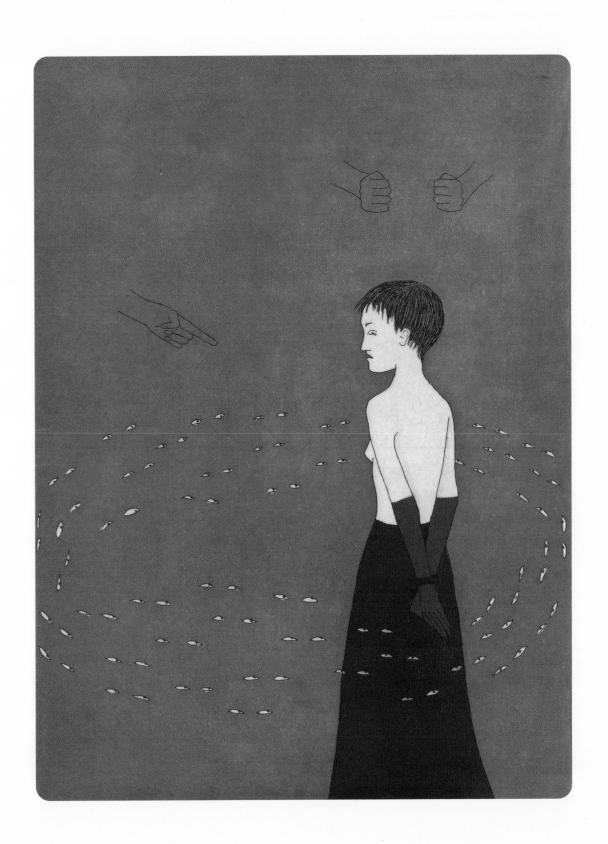

Imprisoned:

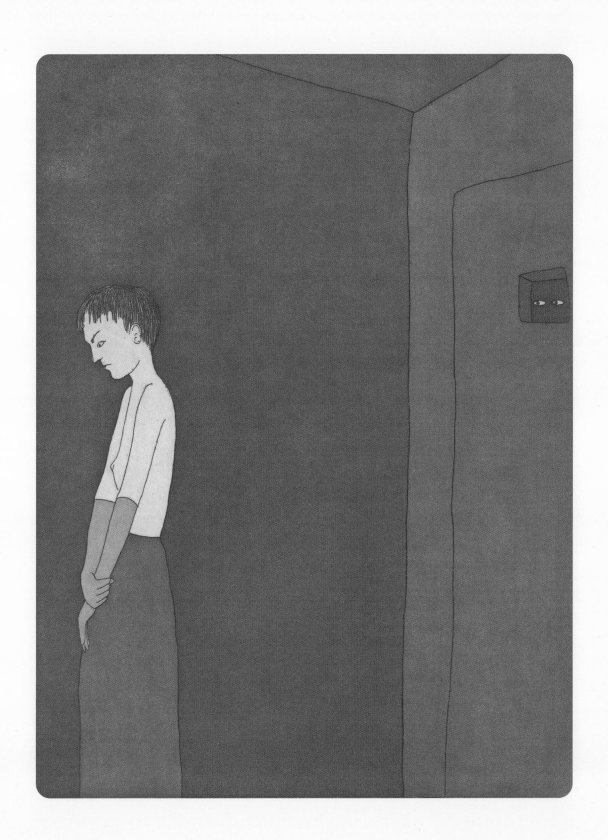

She unraveled her skirt,
Taking it apart thread by thread.
As she did this,
She tied the end of one thread
To the end of the next,
Making a single long thread.

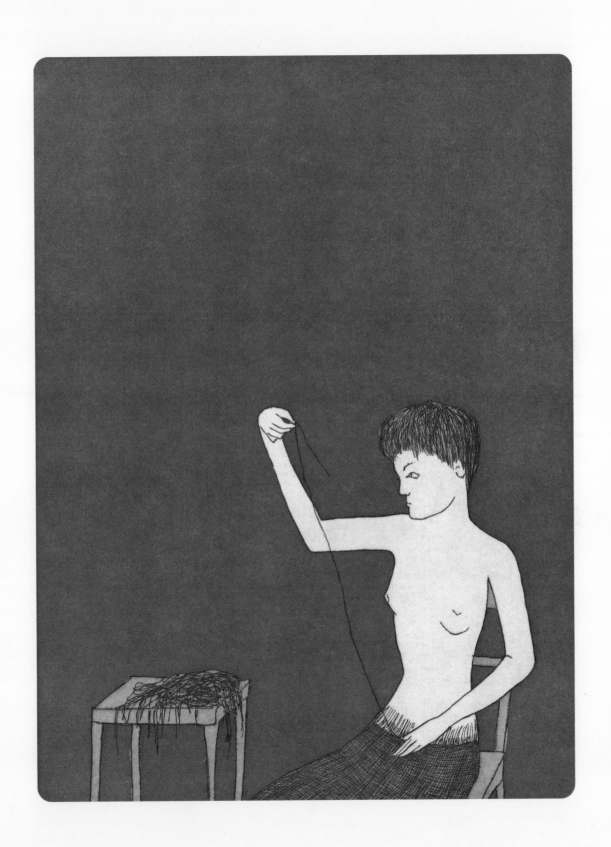

Her arms felt like string.

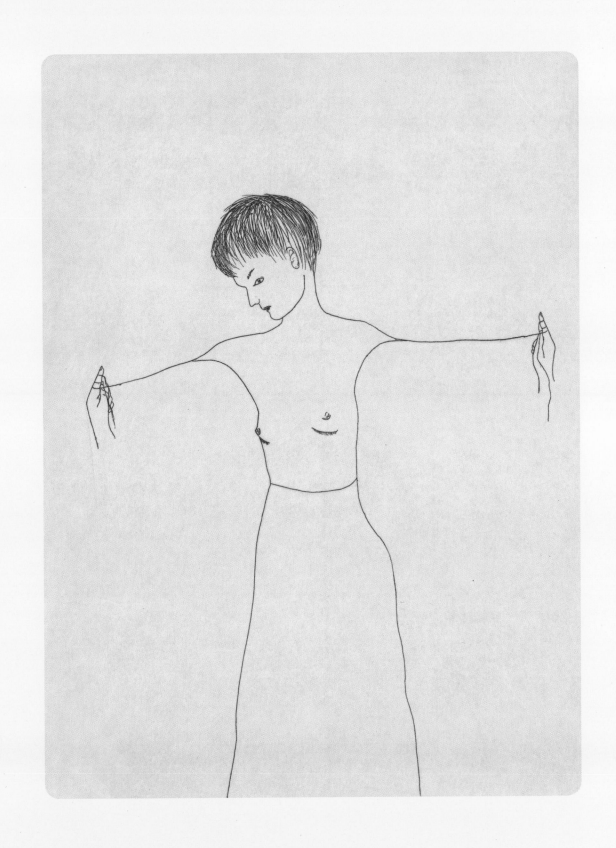

She made a cocoon,
And stayed in it all winter.

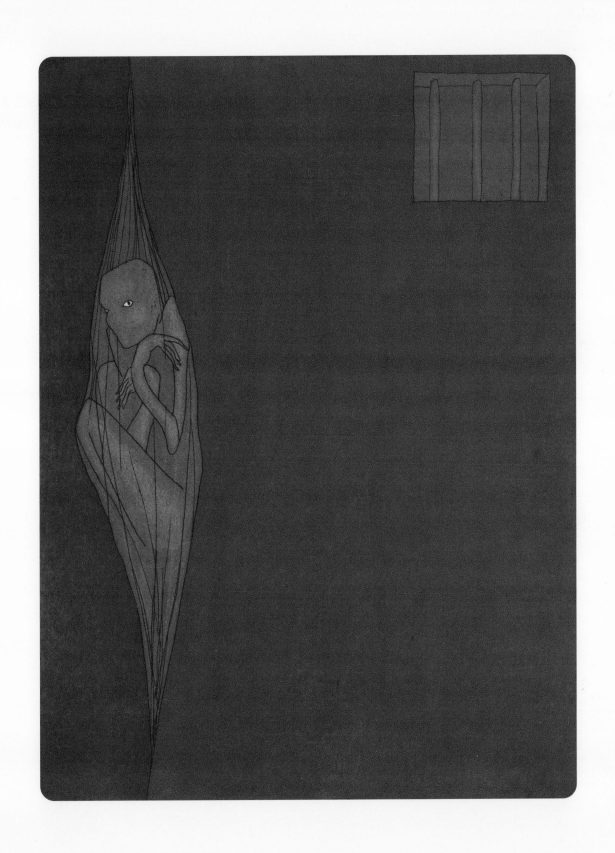

In the spring she emerged as a
Large moth.

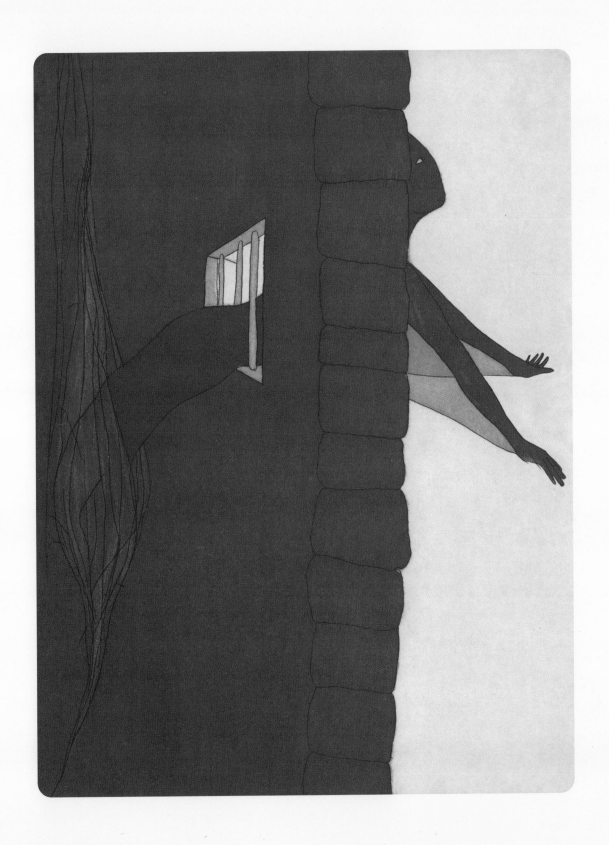

She was an enormous moth,
And she flew until finally,
Exhausted,

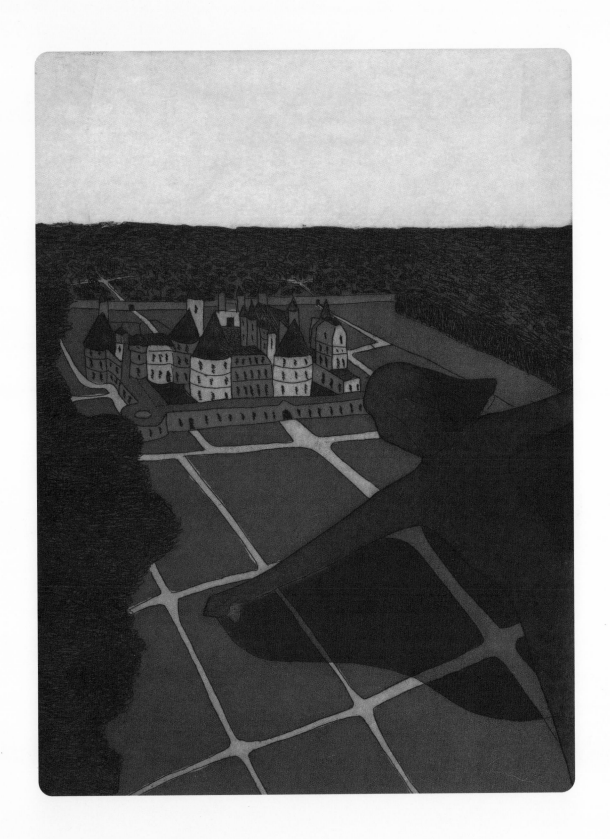

She flew into the garden
Of Napoleon Bonaparte;
He was a butterfly collector
And tried to capture her.

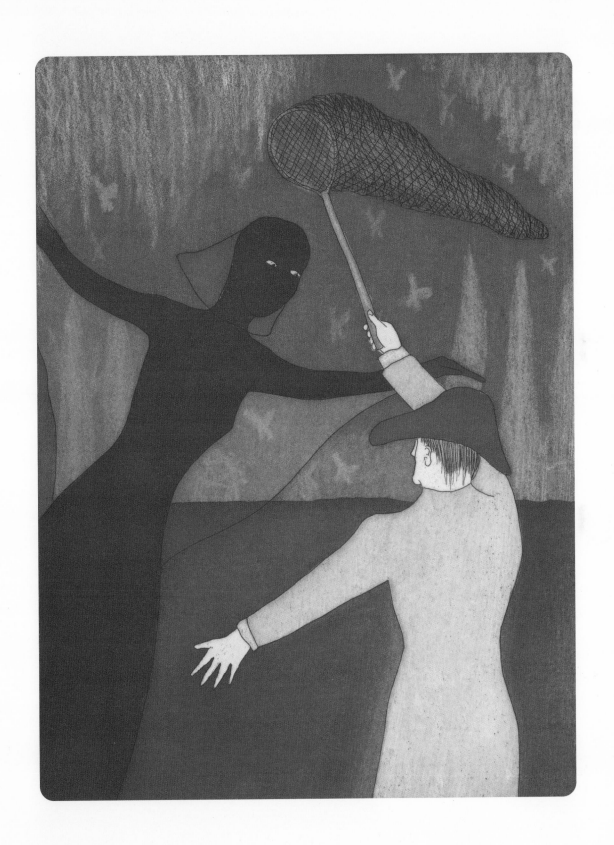

She escaped him
By flying in the library window.

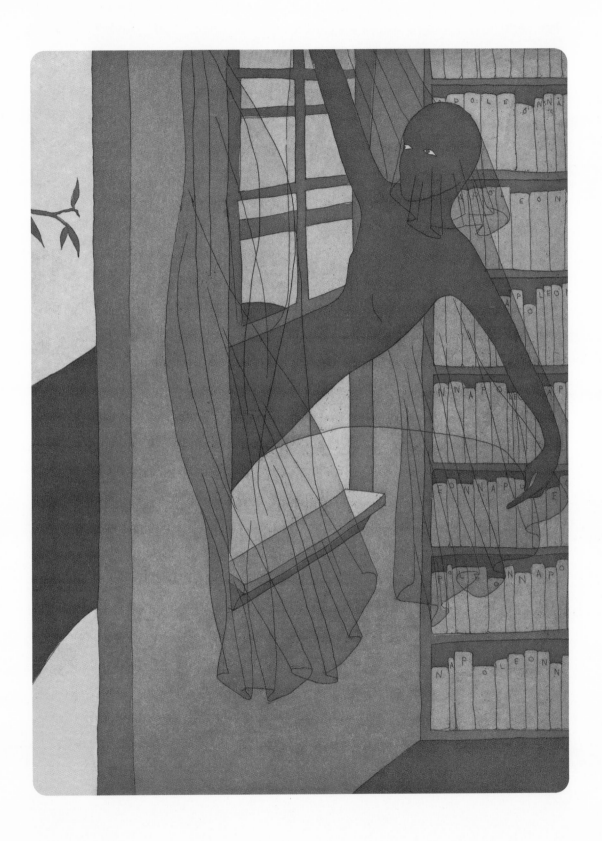

All the books were about Napoleon;
Being a moth, she ate them all.

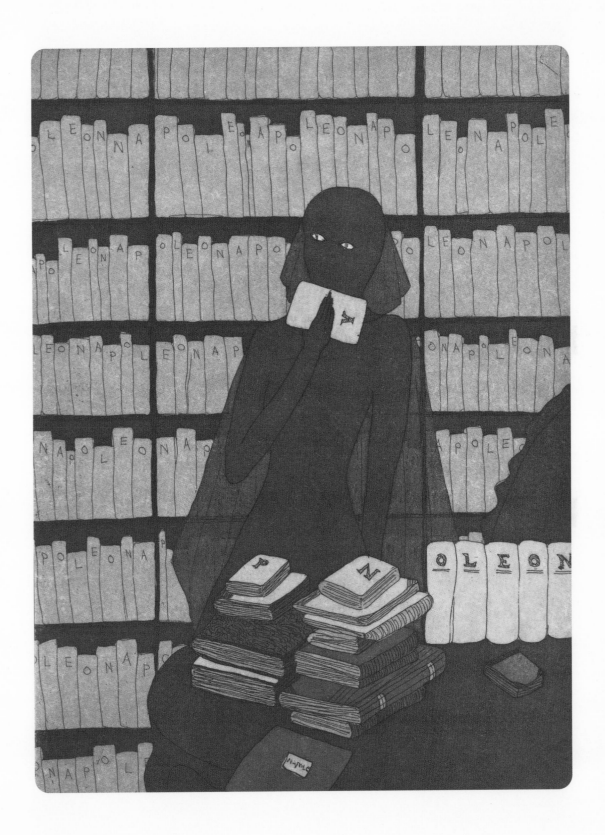

She was returned to herself,
And he found her so:

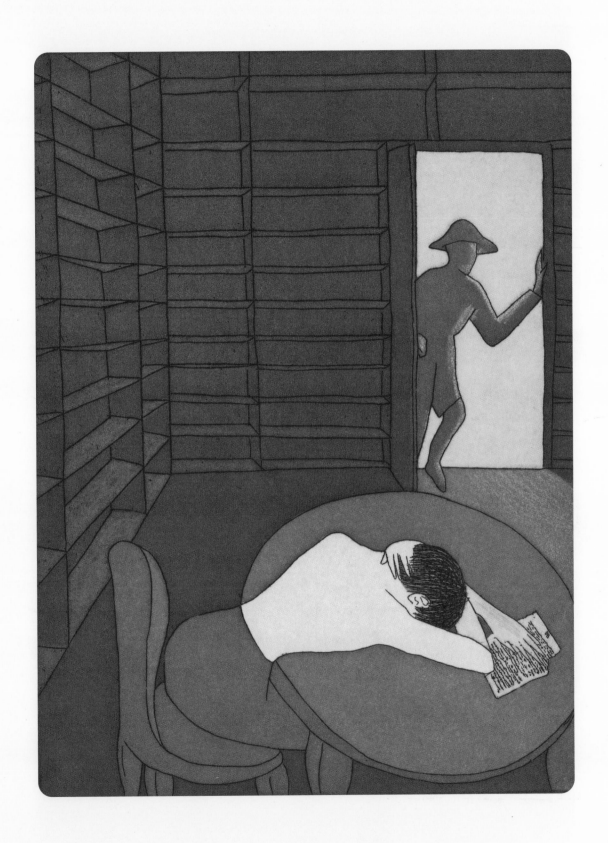

And carried her gently away.

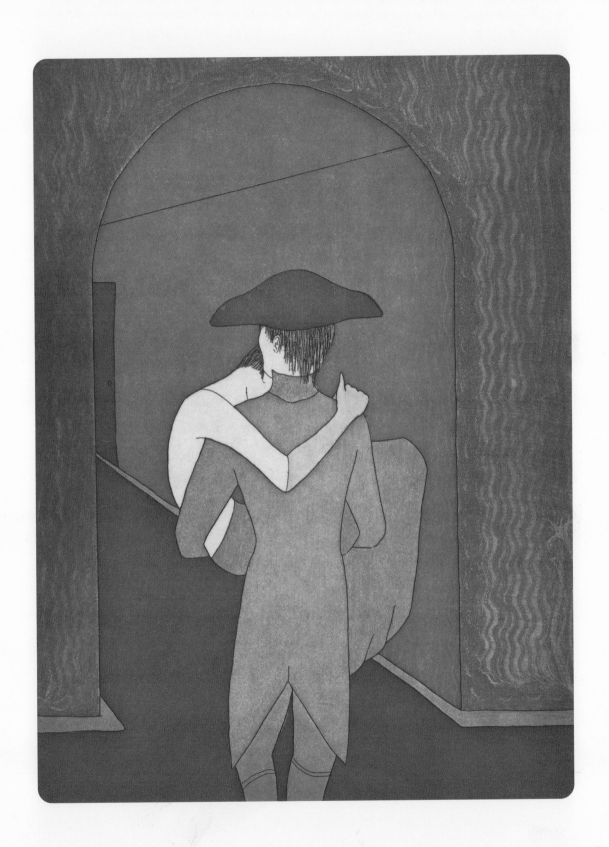

They became lovers.

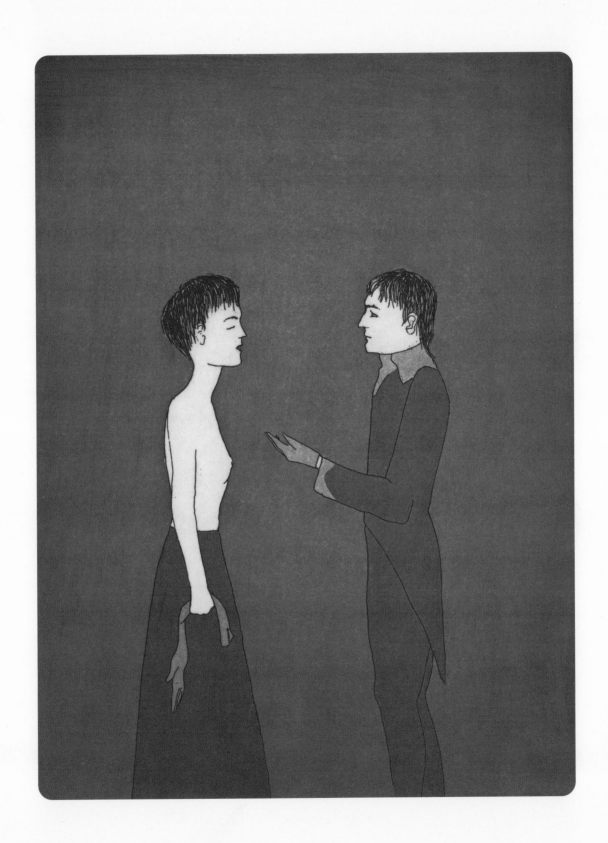

Through the summer
They loved in harmony and joy,

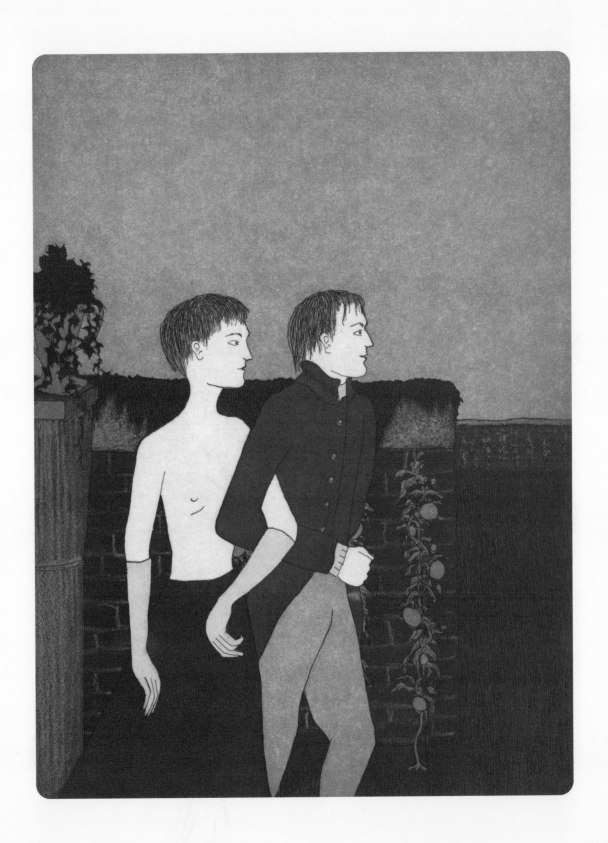

And in the winter
They loved with warmth and good humor.

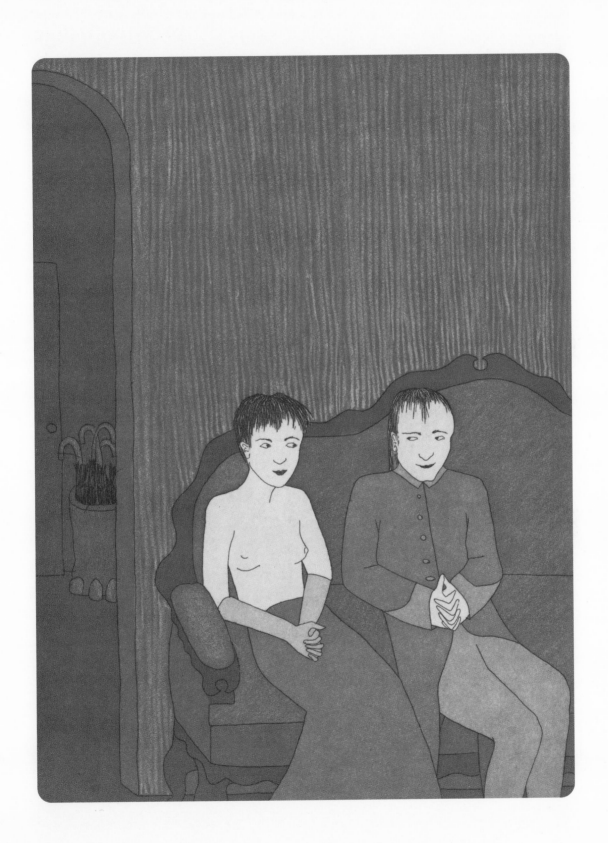

In the spring
Napoleon set off
To conquer Russia.

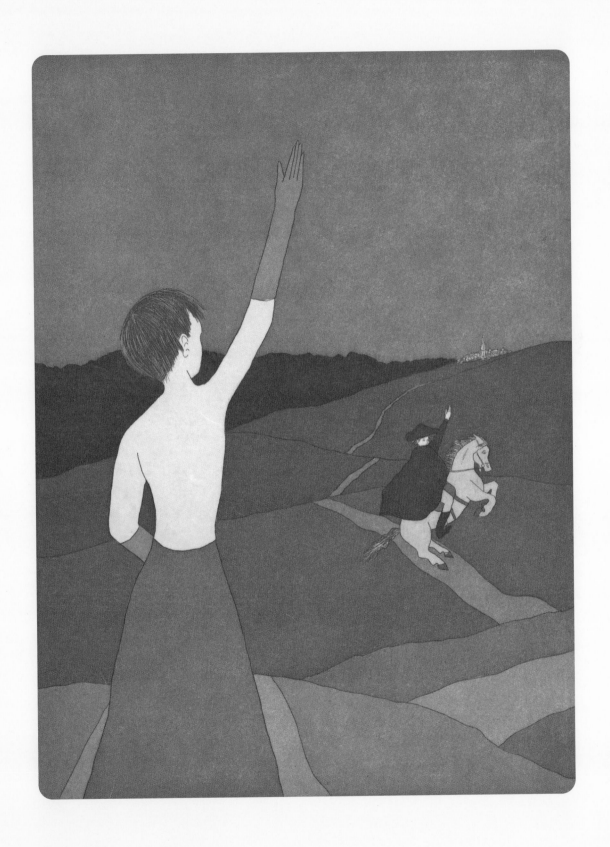

She discovered she was pregnant.

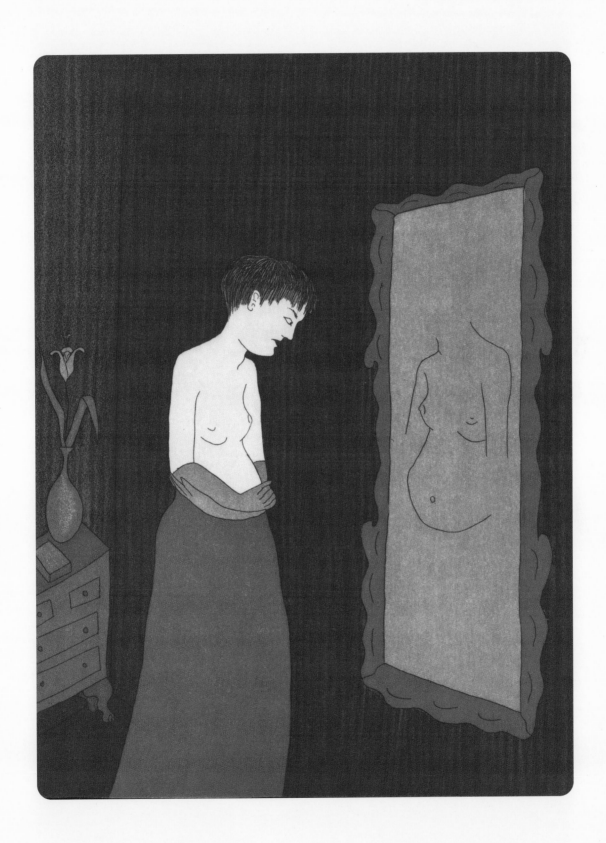

The birth of Maurice:

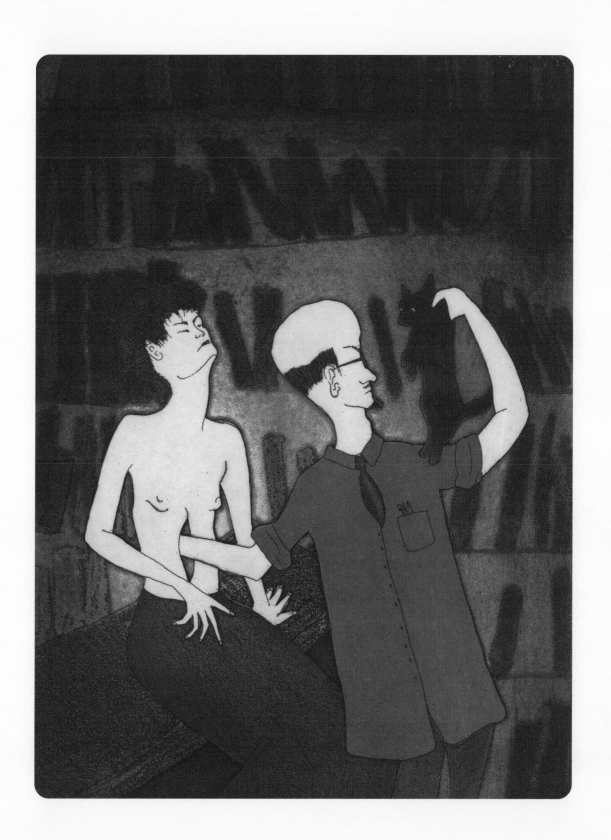

The childhood of Maurice:

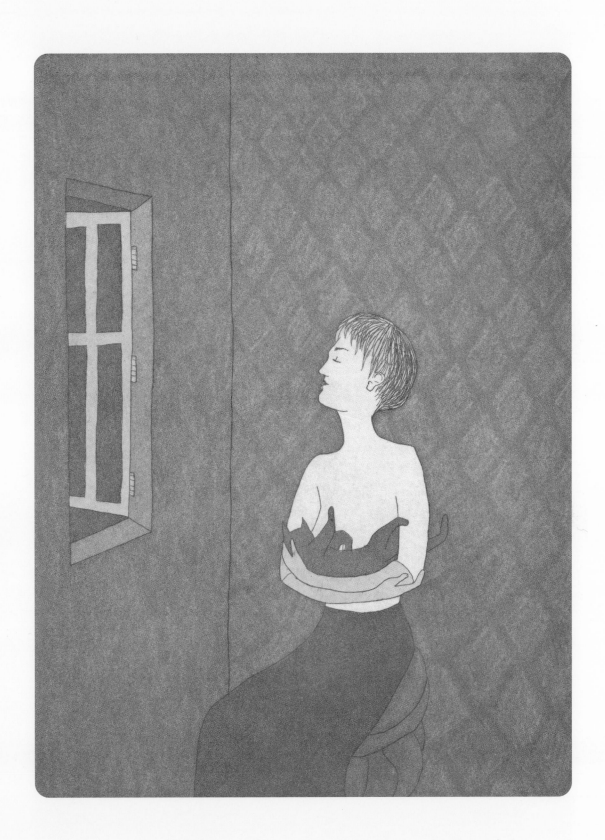

Sometimes,
They sat for hours
In the garden.

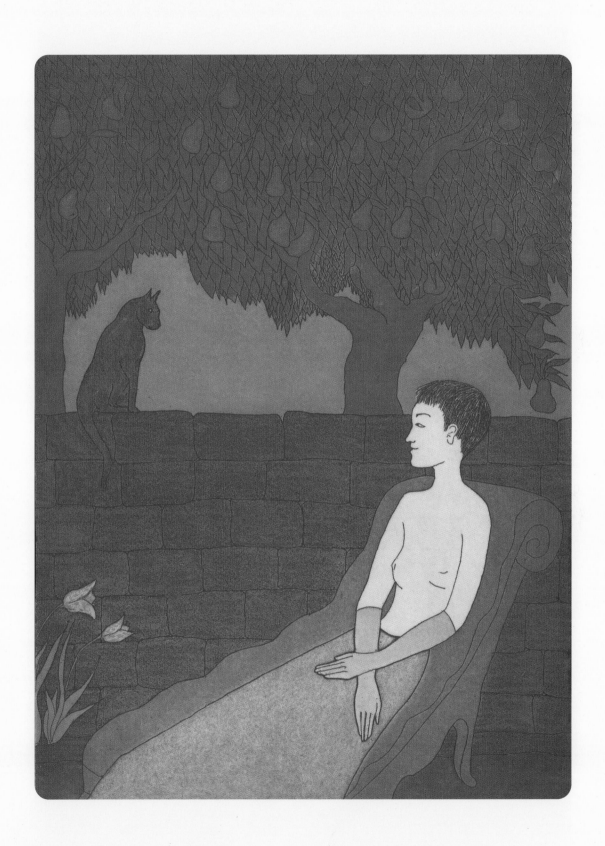

They played together.

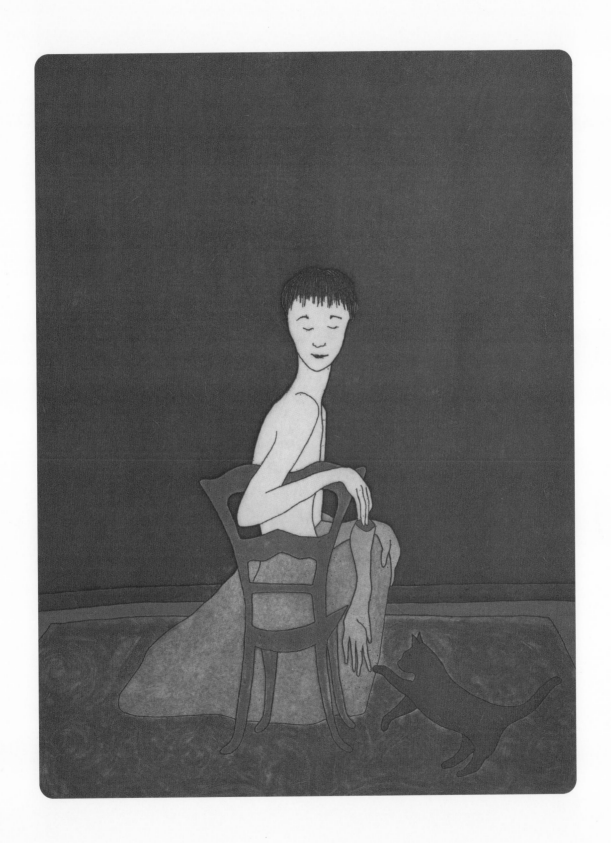

Sometimes,
They simply sat and
Enjoyed each other's company.

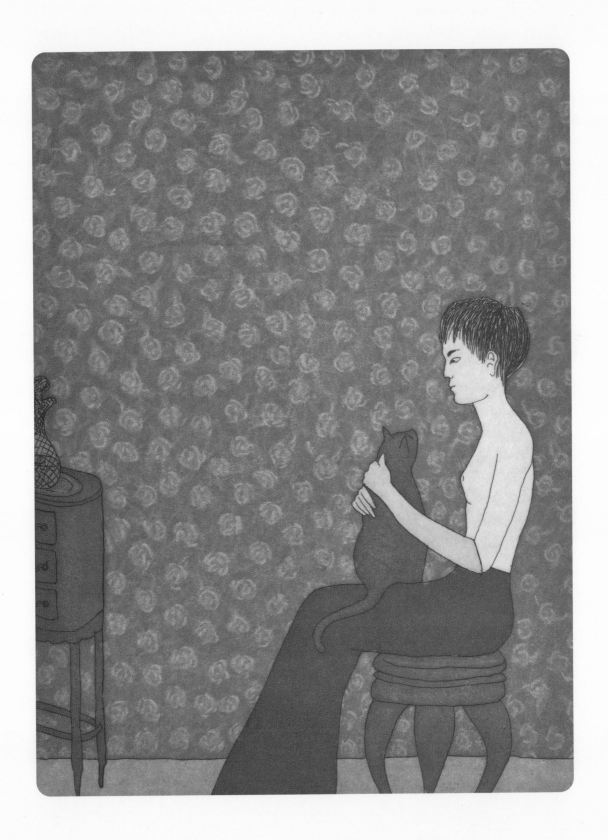

And she waited for Napoleon's return.

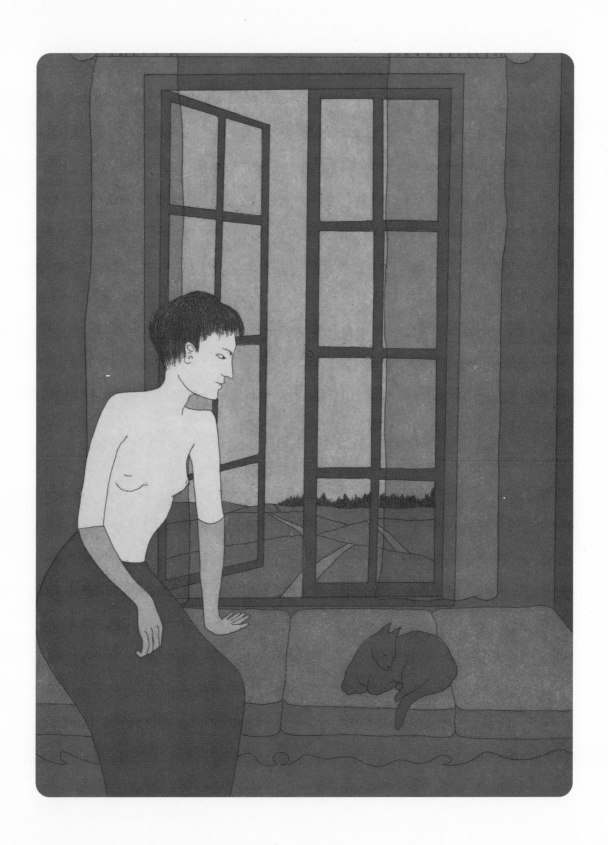

One day an apple seller came,
And in her gossip conveyed that
Napoleon was not in *Russia* at *all*,
But was in the *town*, with a *woman*.

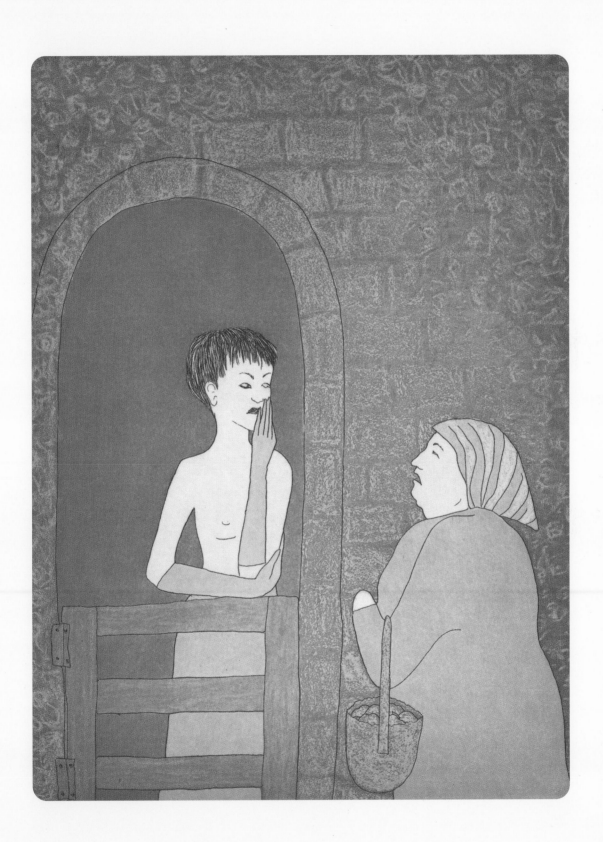

Betrayed.

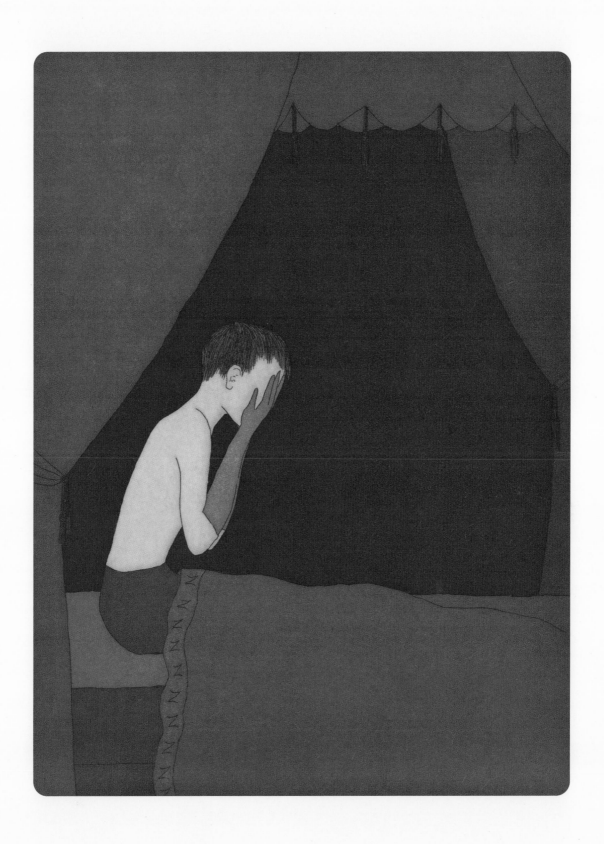

With no thought
Except that she was forsaken,
She left Napoleon's house and Maurice
And went away.

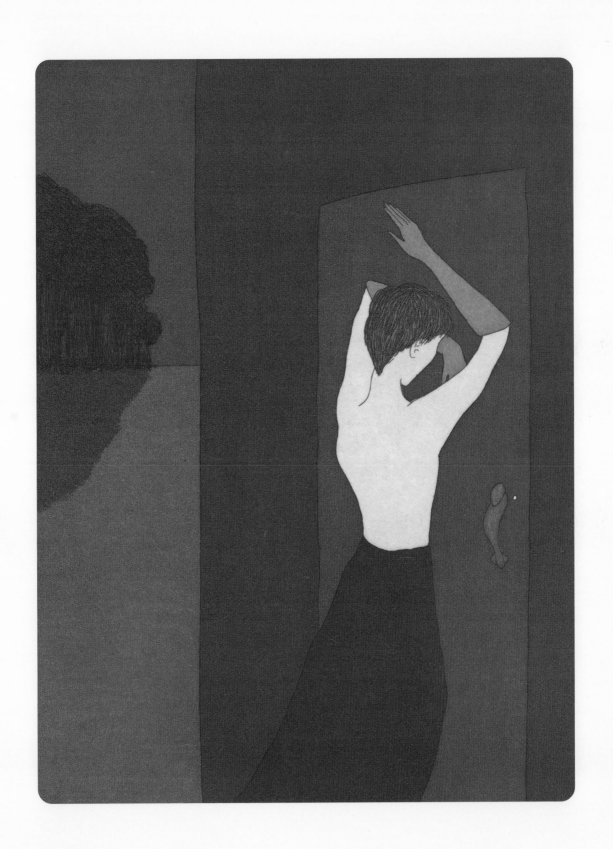

She went into the forest
And wandered there
Until she collapsed,
And was discovered
By a chameleon.

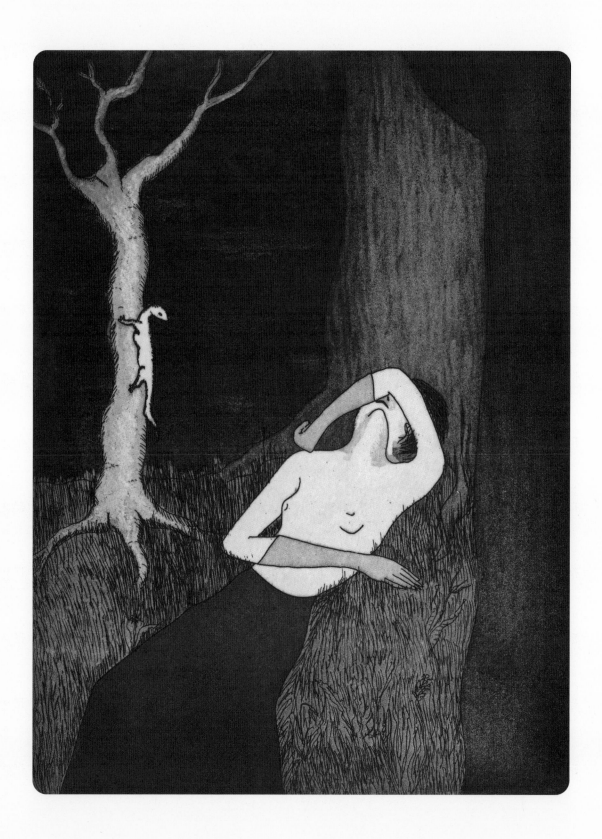

This chameleon, using his own alchemy,
Transformed himself and carried her
Out of the woods to a nunnery
Which stood on a hill.

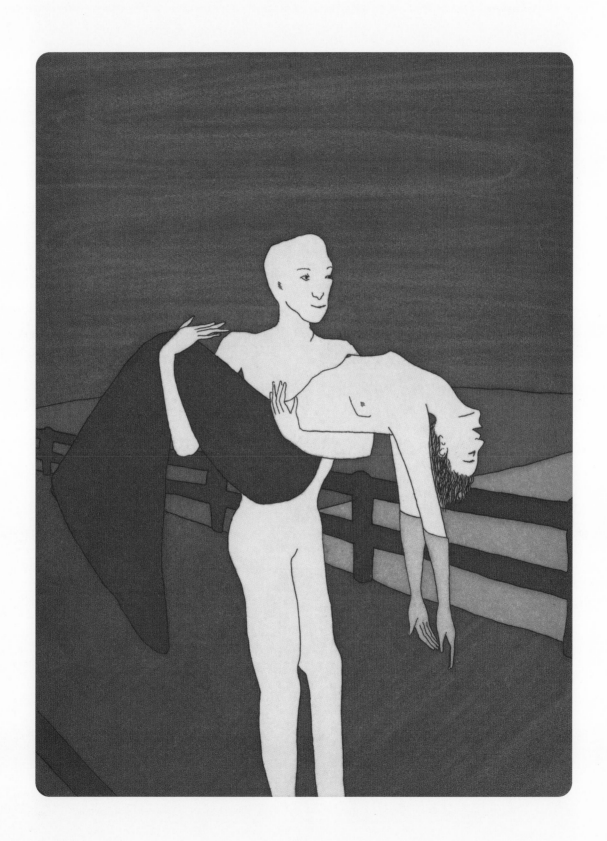

He laid her there,
And when she was taken
Inside by the nuns
He went away.

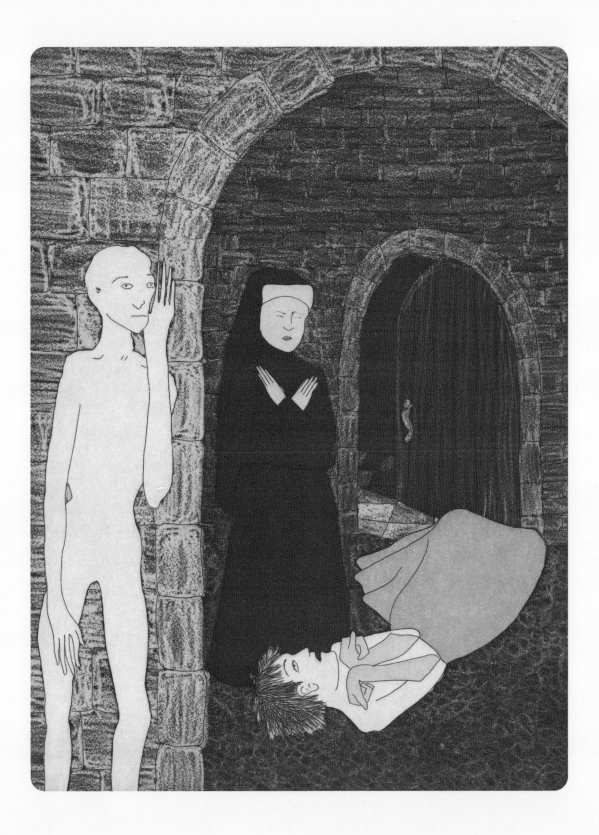

She lay ill.

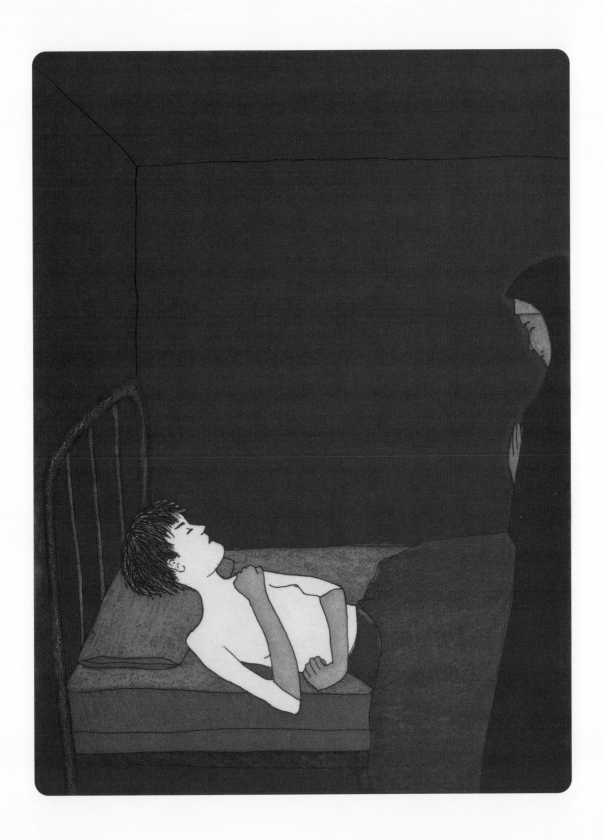

Brain Fever:

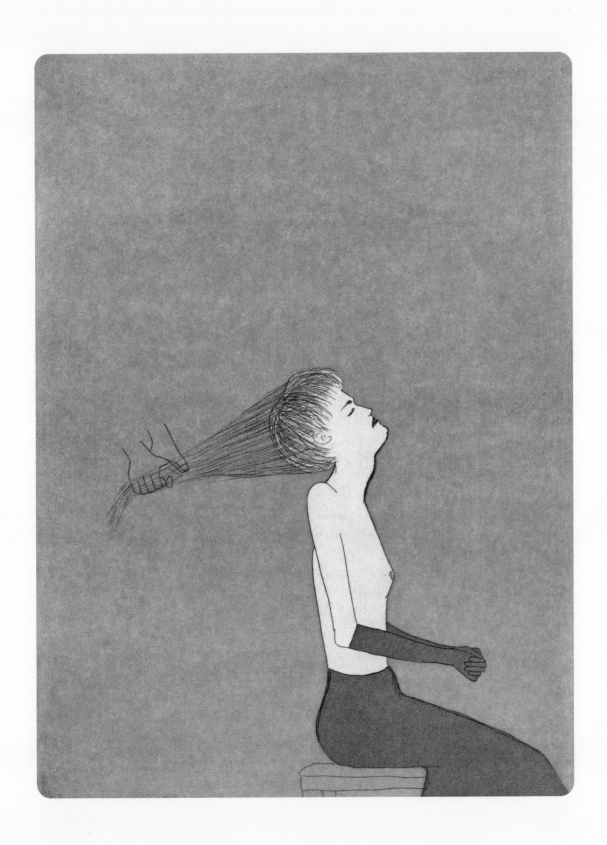

Hallucination:

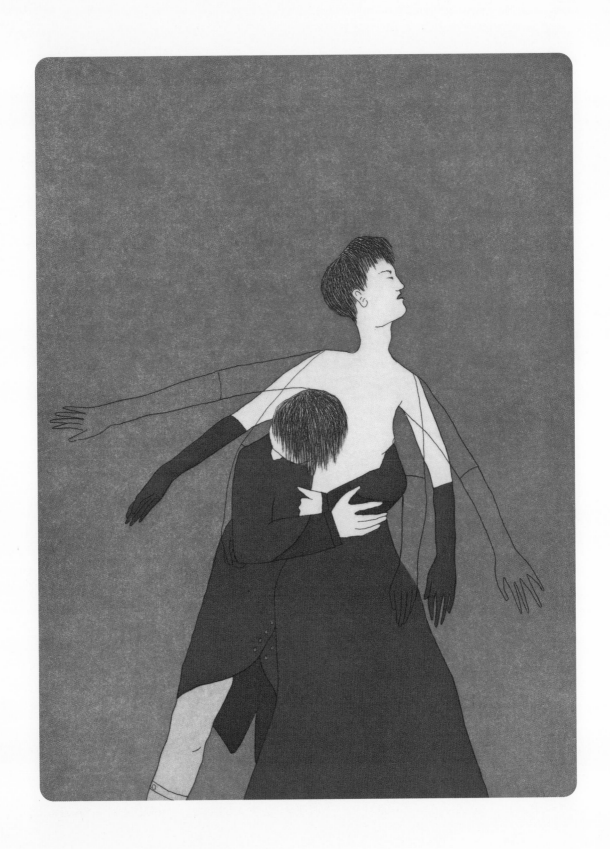

Hallucination:

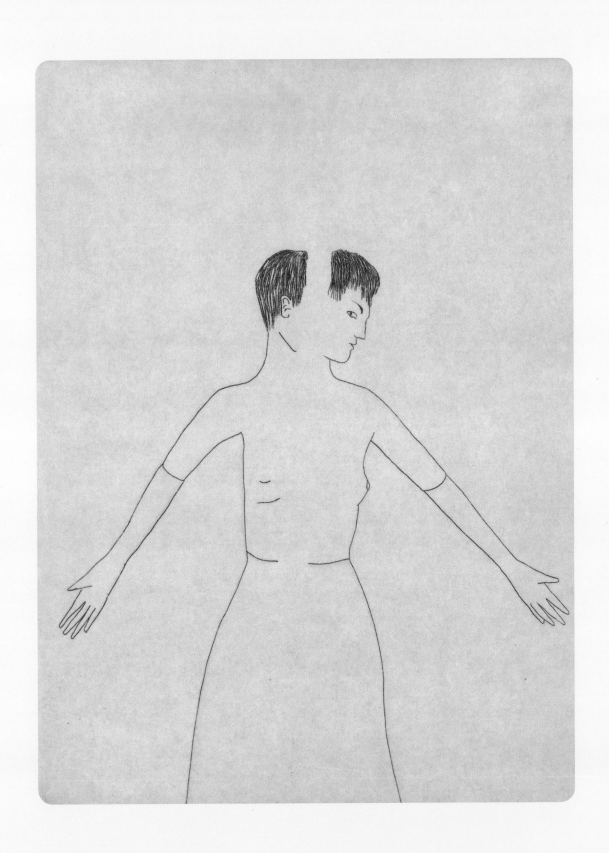

Hallucination:

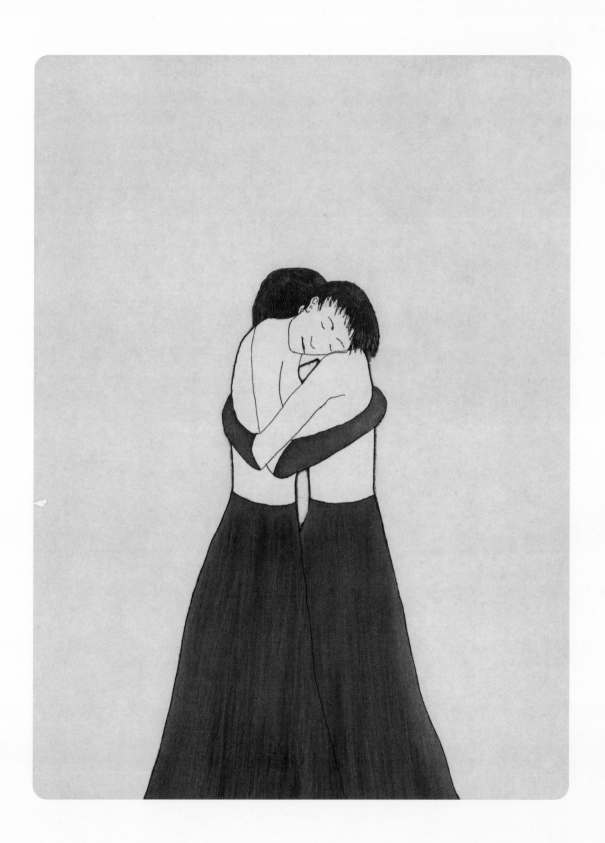

Hallucination:

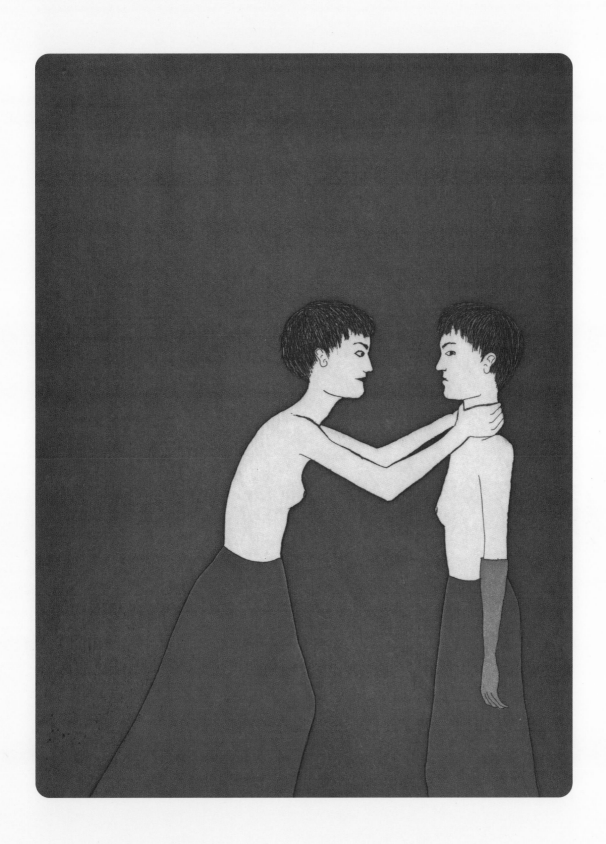

Why?

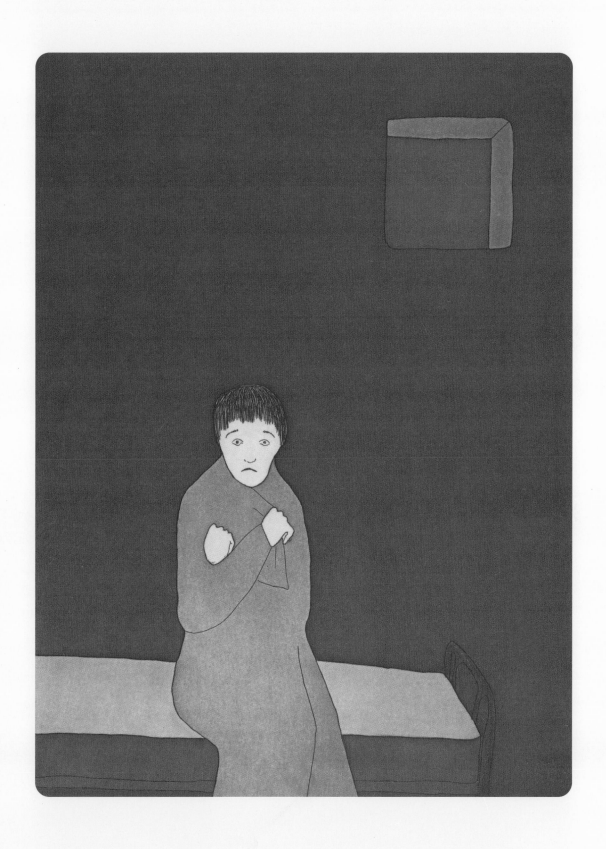

Finally, Maurice found her.

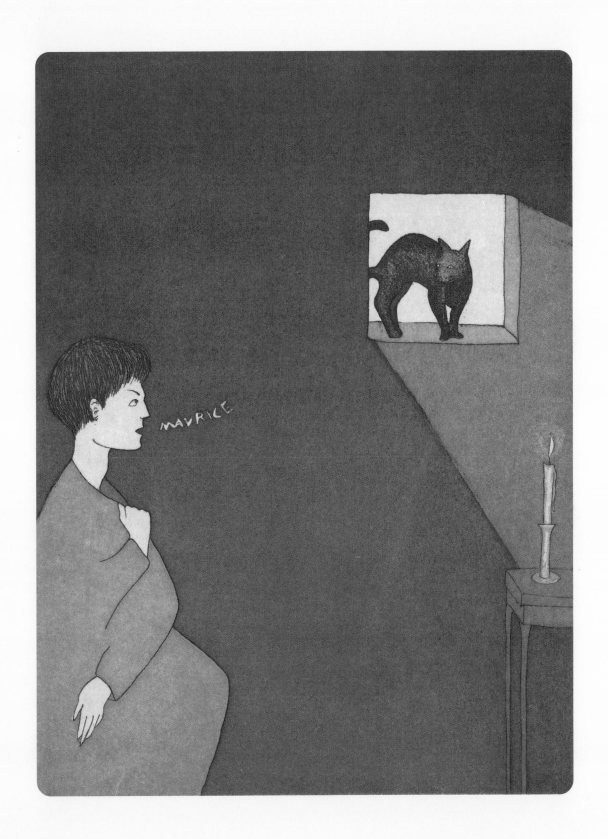

He told her
Of how Napoleon had returned:
Of his sorrow at finding her gone,
And of his remorse.

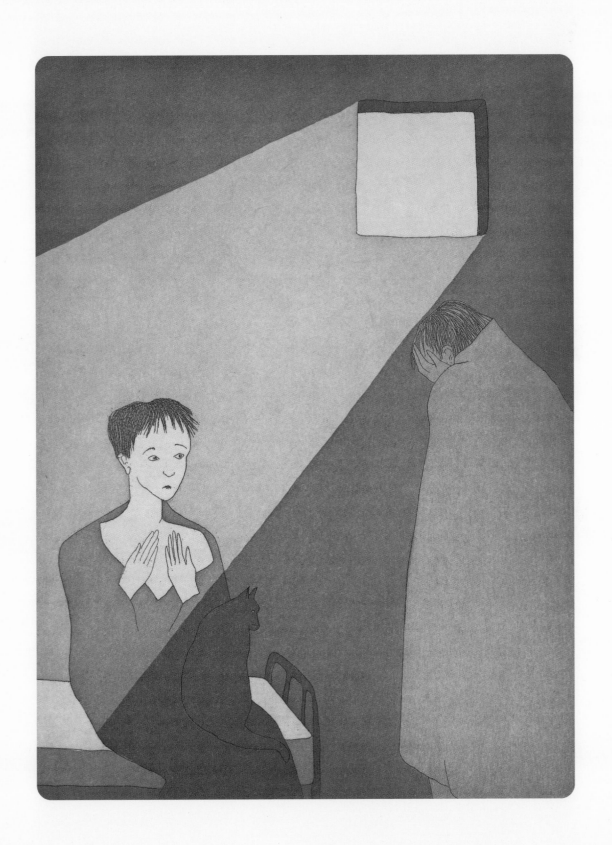

Anguished, she became ill again.

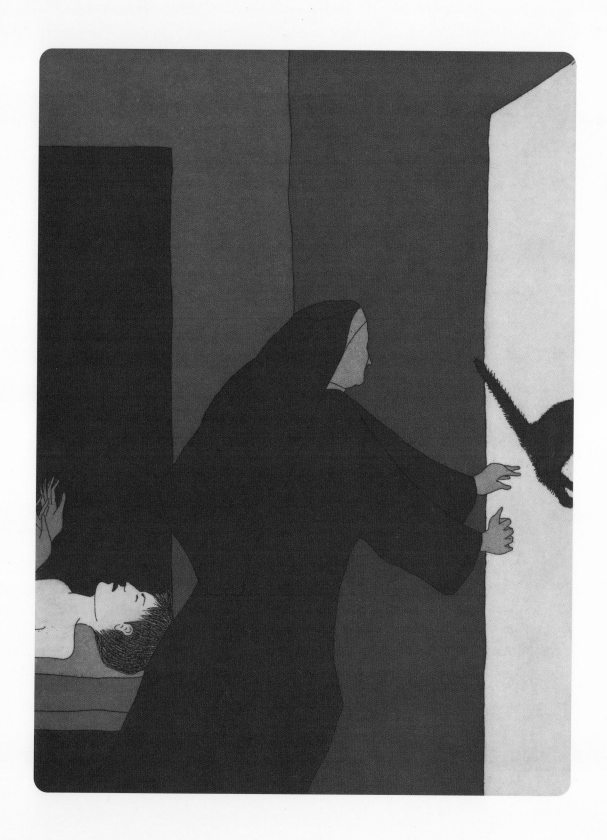

Her death:

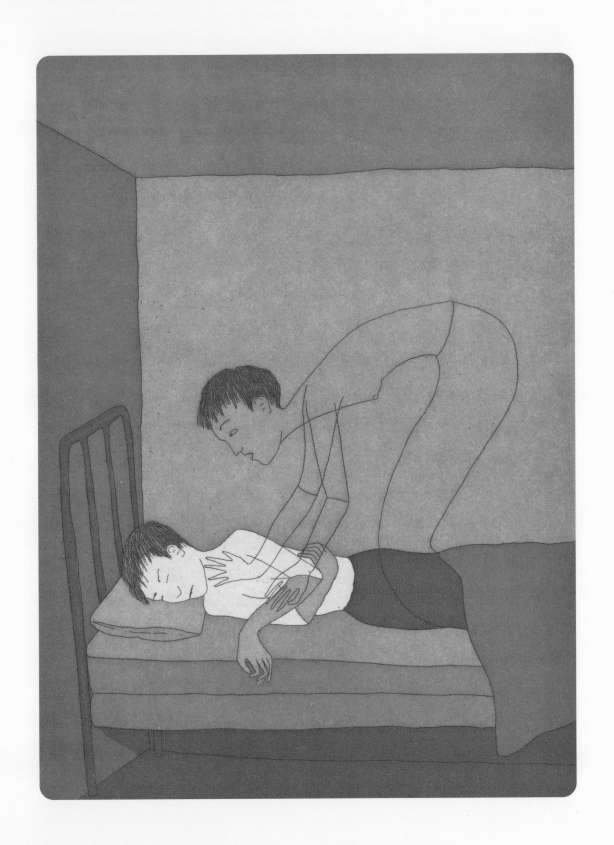

The nuns sang
As they carried her body up the hill.

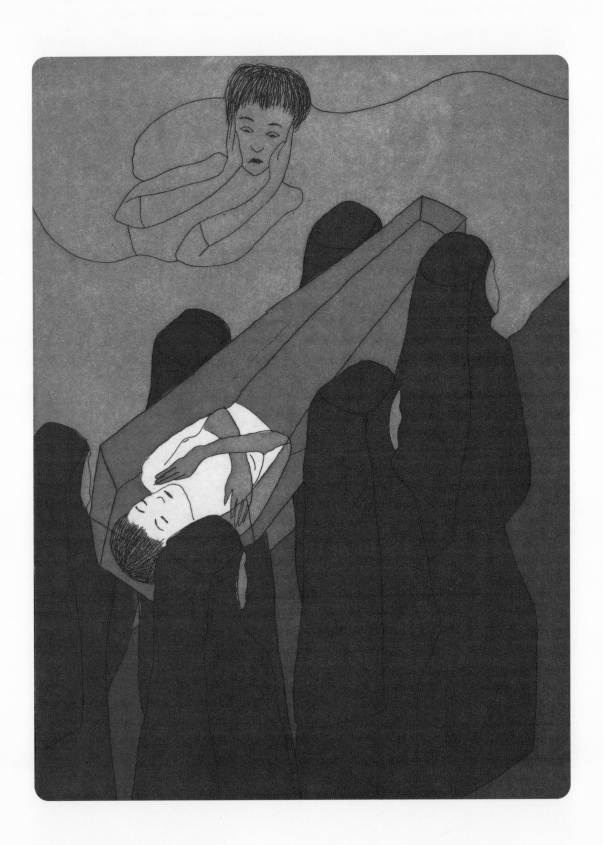

Her spirit mourned for her body.

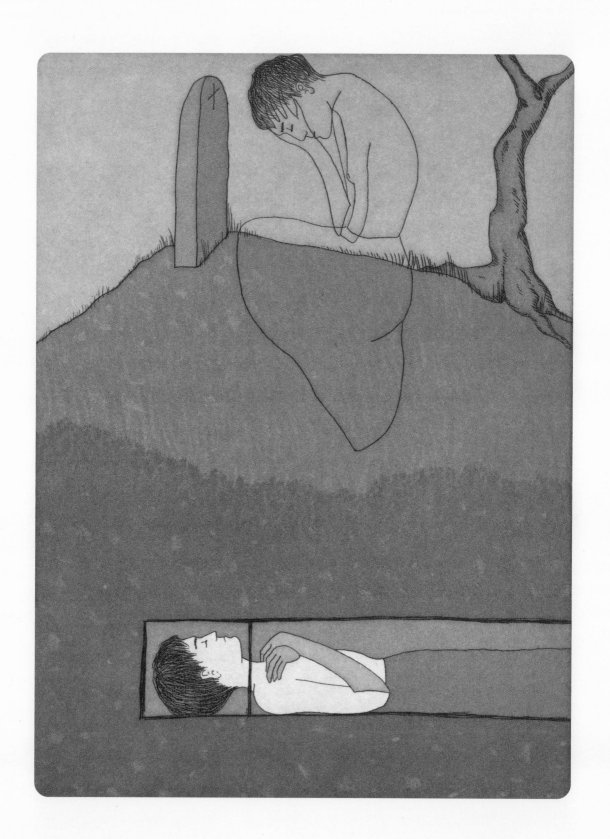

Maurice found her spirit
Wandering in the forest.

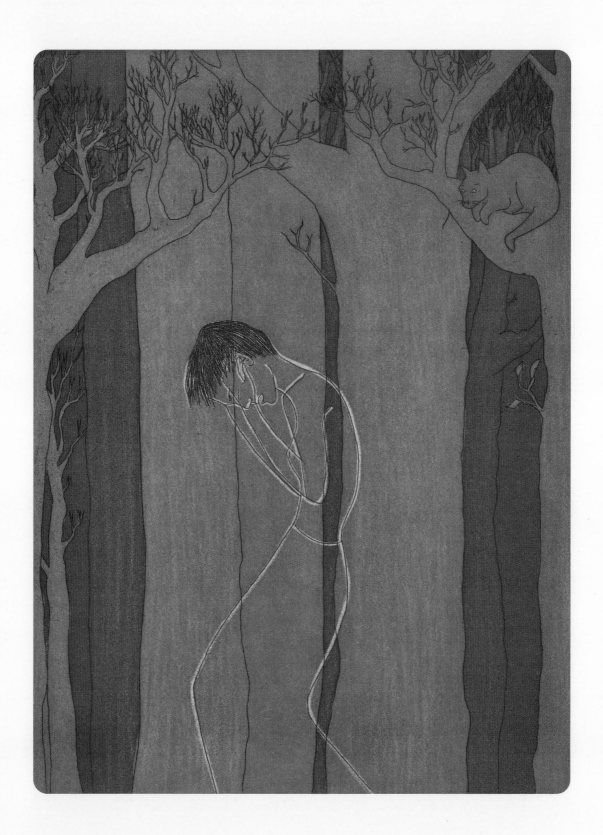

He led her back to Napoleon.

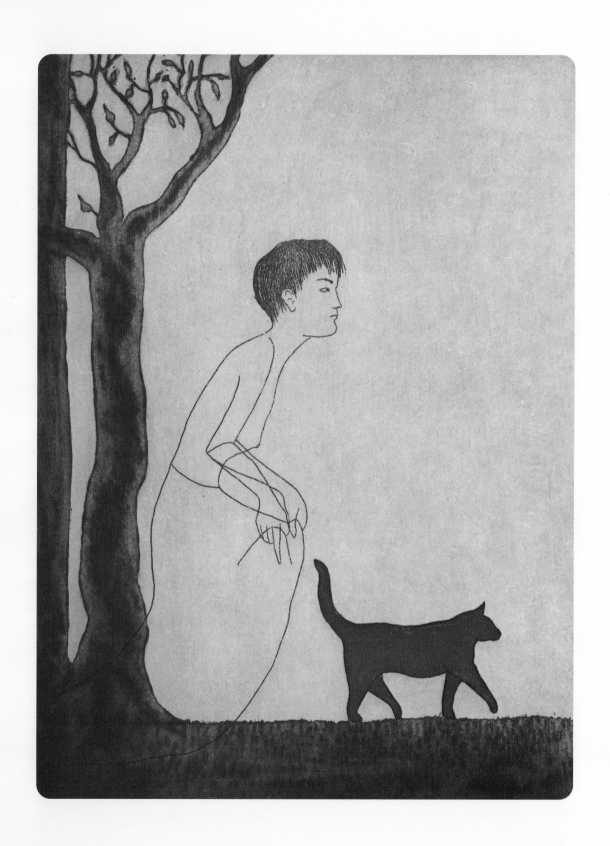

Forgiveness:

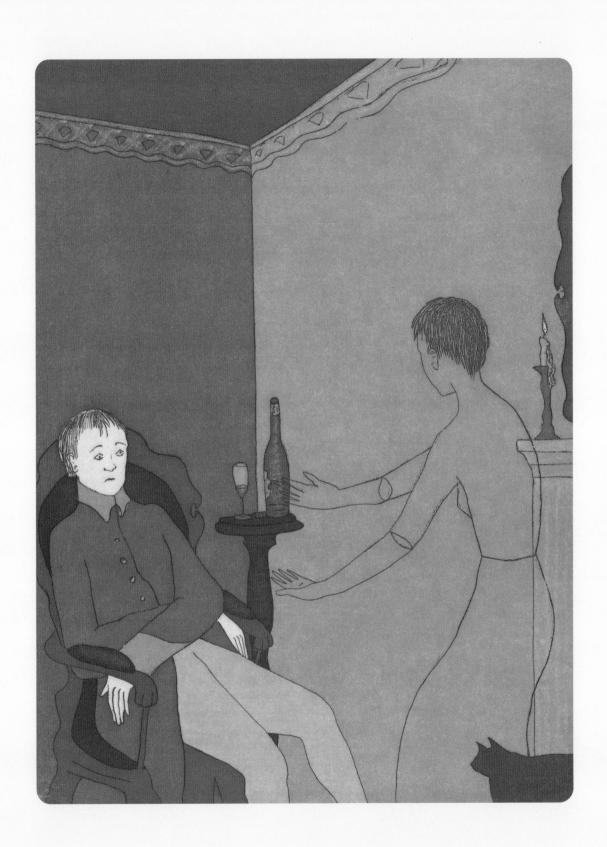

Good-bye.

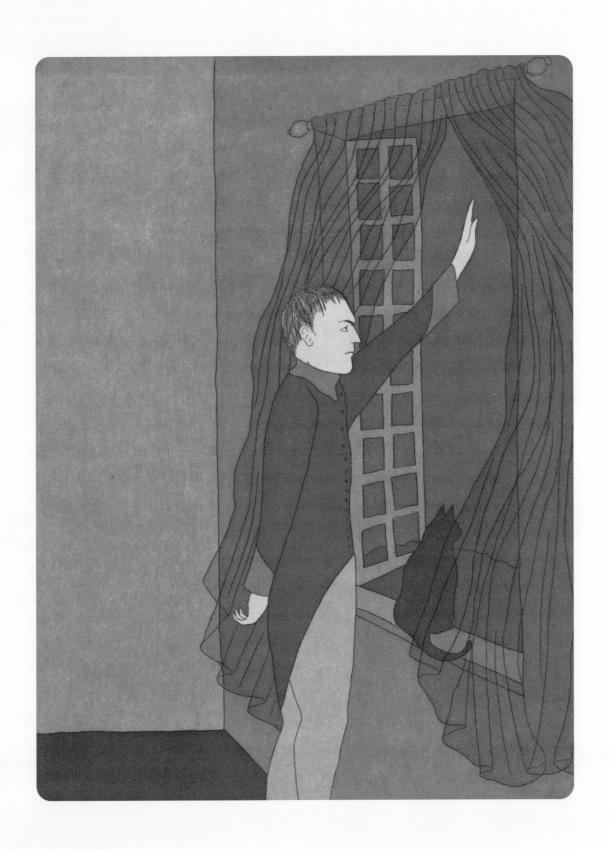

Her spirit flew out into the night
And the sky reached down
And drew her up,
And she was filled with light…

And she is happy.

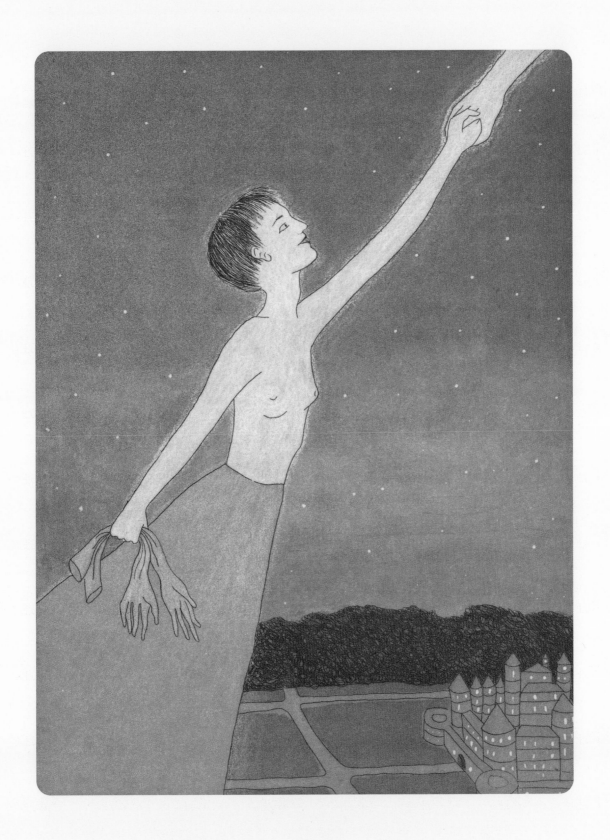

The End

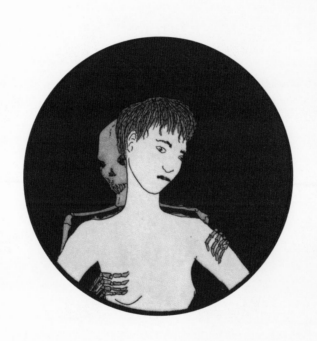

The Adventuress is my first book. I made it between 1983 and 1985, when I was a student at the School of the Art Institute of Chicago. It began with a series of drawings I'd made in my sketchbook: A young woman gives birth to a cat, disguises herself as a giant moth, is tormented by disembodied hands. She is wearing long gloves and a skirt, and nothing else. Who was she? What was going on here? I began to construct a story for her, this strange girl whose fortunes are rather random, who is buffeted by the whim of circumstance like a figure in a dream. The story became this book.

The original books were hand printed and bound in an edition of ten copies. In order to make the books, I learned letterpress printing and bookbinding; many thanks to Ray Martin, Barbara Tetenbaum, and Joan Flasch, my first teachers in those arts. The images themselves are aquatints. These are made by coating a zinc plate with a wax ground, drawing through it with a sharp point, and immersing it in a nitric acid bath. To achieve tonality, the plate is coated with rosin dust, and then blocked out in stages, biting the plate in acid between each stage. The image on the plate is reversed, and hidden by the blockouts, so when the plate is cleaned, inked, and printed for the first time, there's a moment of surprise, recognition, and, with luck, pleasure: The image in the mind's eye suddenly materializes. I am delighted to thank William Wimmer, who first taught me this technique, and to whom I owe a lifetime of prints.

Thanks also to Michael Miller, Mark Pascale, Sidney Block and Bob Hiebert of Printworks Gallery, and Chuck Izui of Aiko's Art Materials. Tamar Brazis of Harry N. Abrams brought this book into its new incarnation with her usual marvelous aplomb, insight, and humor; thanks to Howard Reeves, Michael Jacobs, Andrea Colvin, and Celina Carvalho for their contributions to the publication and design of this book. Thank you to Dan Franklin of Jonathan Cape for help and moral support in all my disparate book projects. Thank you to Joseph Regal, who never sleeps and always listens, who finds homes for all my books.

Last and best, thank you to my family, Patricia, Lawrence, Beth, and Jonelle, for their love and their patience with this wandering girl.

Audrey Niffenegger is a visual artist and writer who lives in Chicago. She has been making books by hand since the early 1980s; more recently she published a novel, *The Time Traveler's Wife*, which was an international bestseller. Miss Niffenegger is currently at work on her second novel, but she's a very slow writer, easily distracted by her cats and the lure of libraries and airplanes.

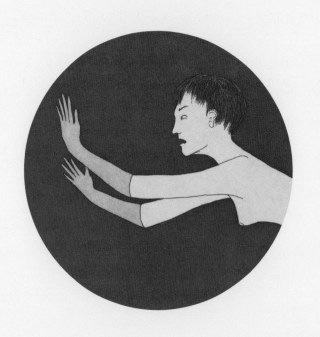